FURY
IN THE
SHADOWS

Books by Rebecca Hemlock

Arctic Mysteries series
Bitter Betrayal
Deadly Decisions

The Granton house series
The Secret of the 14th Room
The Secret Diary of Deadly Deception
Hidden passages to Dark Secrets

Stand alone
Fury in the Shadows

"That the trial of your faith, being much more precious than of gold that perisheth, though it be tried with fire, might be found unto praise and honour and glory at the appearing of Jesus Christ"

I Peter 1:7 KJV

FURY
IN THE
SHADOWS

REBECCA
HEMLOCK

CHAPTER 1

April 2019
3:45pm

Jessica Everett knocked on the door of the rundown trailer as she flipped through the manilla file in her hand. Her mind replayed the routine questions she always asked when making house calls.

Are you doing okay? When was the last time your husband was on the property?

She scanned through the file to learn what she was dealing with. *Annabelle Mason. A case of physical abuse from a significant other, resulting in broken bones.* It was cases like this that made her blood boil. She'd known an Annabelle once. A long time ago. As a social worker for the Oakwood Springs Crisis Center, it was her job to check in on the women she had successfully helped get away from their abusive husbands and boyfriends. Some days she felt like a hero, and others, she felt like a disapproving parent of a runaway teen.

Beads of sweat popped up on Jess's neck. She grabbed the elastic band that held her black hair in a ponytail and yanked it higher. The height of her hair relieved some of the heat but did little to release her nerves. Of course, it wasn't as if she had no idea why she was nervous. But that was silly. There was no way this was *that* Annabelle.

It didn't matter anyway. That Annabelle would never speak to her again. She wasn't even supposed to be here. She was only handling this case because her friend, Mia, was on vacation, and she promised to cover some of her cases for her. A decision she was quickly regretting.

She stood on the porch steps waiting for someone to come to the door. The tiny home seemed clean on the outside. Pine trees surrounded the trailer, making it difficult to see very far into the woods that wrapped around the house.

Before she could knock a second time, a loud crash sounded from inside. Alarm coursed through her. She ignored her instincts to get inside her car and call 911.

Annabelle Mason might be hurt and need her help. Jess pushed the door open and peeked inside—something her job only allowed if she felt the need to check on things.

Annabelle should've come to the door already. Something wasn't right. Dealing with victims of domestic violence was what she did best, but she wasn't about to let it happen when she could do something. A small whimper came from the kitchen.

"Hello? It's Jess from the Oakwood Springs Crisis Center. Is everything alright here?"

She tiptoed through the living room and found herself surrounded by dark red walls and tiny windows; the last thing she would've chosen for home décor if she lived here. A shiver ran up her spine.

She entered the kitchen, coming to a sudden stop. Her breath instantly caught in her throat. A young woman with long red hair lay on the floor. She had blood trickling down her chest from what looked like a stab wound. Jess dropped to her side and lifted her torso, bringing Annabelle's face closer to hers. Their eyes met.

"Jess," Annabelle whispered. The color drained from Jess's face as she realized this *was* that Annabelle. That one she'd known as a child. The warmth of her body pulsed with what life she had left.

"It's okay. You're gonna be alright." Jess had to keep her calm. She reached for a dish towel crumpled on the counter and pressed it into the wound. Holding it there, she tried to remember everything she was supposed to do in an emergency. *Don't try to move her. Stop the bleeding and call 911.* She instructed Annabelle to hold the dishtowel to her chest. Her now free hand went to her back pocket, patting it for her phone. She pulled it out and tapped the numbers as fast as possible, then pressed it to her ear.

A slight creak from the floor whined behind her. She froze, the hairs on her arm rising to attention. She and Annabelle weren't the only ones here. Jess's breath caught in her throat. She was in such a frenzy to help Annabelle that the possibility of the attacker still being in the house was in the very back of her mind.

Two eyes burned through the back of her neck. The attacker was waiting for her to make one wrong move. It could be only a matter of time before she was lying on the floor next to Annabelle.

Jess imagined a vicious beast standing behind her, covered in blood, clutching a big kitchen knife. She laid Annabelle back down on the floor. Sliding the phone in her front pocket. She managed to dial 911, but she'd be dead before they arrived. She could faintly hear the dispatcher's voice and prayed they wouldn't hang up.

Her father's favorite saying echoed in her mind. "Better make sure you're good with the man upstairs. Every day could be your last." This was one day he could be right.

As Jess slowly stood, she clenched her jaw. Deep down, she knew she was ready to die in the spiritual sense, but for Annabelle's sake, she wasn't going to die without a fight. She balled her fists and swung around as quickly as she could. Her right hand met an ear.

A man's voice growled in pain as a fist collided with her stomach. Jess doubled over, her eyes wide as the wind left her lungs with a grunt. Two strong arms wrapped around her waist, pinning her arms to her sides. She ground her heel into the toe of his white tennis shoes as hard as she could. Whipping her body back, she headbutted him with all her strength.

She twisted herself free from his grasp and bolted. A feeling of dread and guilt filled her for leaving Annabelle behind, but she had a better chance of helping her if she was alive. Footsteps pounded the floor behind her. She burst out the door, giving it a firm slam. She leaped off the porch, hearing something hit the ground with a tinkle before she landed. A quick slap of her thigh told her it was her car keys. There was no way now she could use her car to escape. She inwardly kicked herself for not buying a lanyard the last time her keys fell out of her pocket.

God, please help me. She had no idea where she was running to or if she could outrun this man. It took her several minutes to drive out here from town. She would have to run about two and a half miles before reaching the first house for help. Her phone was still in her pocket, and she wished she was able to call 911, but slowing down even a little could result in her being captured and killed. Hopelessness began to settle on her.

She was tempted to look over her shoulder to get a look at the man's face just in case she did make it out of this alive. Jess ran down the small paved road, then ducked into a thick part of the woods. Maybe she could find a place to hide. Maybe he would give up looking for her. She leaped over a fallen tree and dodged a large branch that hung low.

God, help me out of this. She prayed again, feeling like God hadn't heard her the first time because she was still running from this coldblooded murderer.

She caught sight of a thick bush with an opening small enough for a baby deer to get into. She dove under the bush. Placing her hand over her mouth did very little to silence her panting. She hoped that scrunching in a fetal position would keep the pounding of her heart quiet. What if he found her? What if these were her last minutes alive?

The silhouette of a man in a baseball cap moved back and forth a few feet from the bush. The brim of his cap turned one way, then the other, looking for any indication of which way she could've gone. She tensed all her muscles, forcing them to be still. Her body began to ache from being motionless. Her calves burned. The man in the baseball cap stood near the bush for several seconds. Tears ran down her face at the thought of being captured. She'd always been called a fighter, but could she really do that when it came down to it? Would she survive?

"Are you lost?" Another man's voice came from her left.

"No, sir. I'm just looking for my girlfriend. She likes to play hide and seek," a deep gravelly voice responded.

"Well, I've been out here all morning, and I haven't seen anyone."

"It's alright. She's probably already made it back to the car. I *will* find her." His words were meant for her. He must've figured she was somewhere nearby.

Her heart hammered even faster. If he found her car, he would soon know her name and home address. He would find where she lived and kill her.

"Well, have a good morning then, and keep off my property in the future." The first voice was firm, but something was familiar about it. A voice she hadn't heard in years.

Memories of all the times she'd heard that voice flashed in her mind's eye. Michael Redman? What was her high school sweetheart doing here?

The capped figure turned and slowly walked away. Jess kept her hand over her mouth. She was so afraid that she would start crying from how close she'd come to death.

"You can come out now," the voice said.

She stayed still.

"No, really. He's gone, and I can smell your perfume."

Jess's insides tightened. She had no idea if this person was Michael or someone that sounded a lot like him. Maybe she just hoped it was him because she yearned for that perfectly safe feeling she used to have when she was with him. Before he'd shattered her heart. That reminded her of something they had to tell the girls at the Crisis Center. *Remembering what the person was like before the abuse started doesn't justify who they are now or how badly they treat you.* Michael never laid a hand on her in any way, but the day he told her he was marrying someone else might as well have been a stab to the chest with a knife. A wound that ached to this day.

The bush rustled around her as the toe of a brown leather boot nearly kicked her in the face. The familiar figure kicked the bush a few more times.

"C'mon out. I know you're in there."

"Alright! Alright! I'm coming out." She wasn't sure what to expect when she was back out in plain sight. But she balled up her fists so tightly that her knuckles turned white. She was ready to fight a grizzly bear if need be.

Jess crawled out of her hiding place, despite everything inside her screaming to stay put. Her eyes traveled up from the cowboy boots, and jeans to the face of a man who sort of looked like Michael Redman, but older and without that boyish charm she used to find so attractive.

"Jess? What in the world!" His head jerked back. Eyes big as saucers. He grabbed her arm to help her to her feet.

Tears ran down her face. "Call the police and an ambulance! That man stabbed someone in the trailer down that way." She pointed in the direction she'd run from.

"Hang on." He pulled his phone from his pocket, dialed, and placed it to his ear. "This is Deputy Redman."

Jess took in more of his appearance as he detailed their situation to the emergency operator. A shotgun was shoved under his arm, and a camo hat sat across his shiny black hair.

"Got it," He pressed the red button on his phone, quickly shoving it back into his pocket. He grabbed her arm once again and pulled her in the opposite direction of the trailer.

"Where are we going? Annabelle is that way!" Jess pulled him back toward the trailer.

"An ambulance is on its way there right now, along with two police officers. I need to get you to safety *now!*"

*****

Michael kept a firm grip on Jess's arm. Jess. She was the last person he'd expected to bump into. This version of her looked slightly older than the girl he left crying in her dorm room when he called her to tell her things were over between them. That young girl, who used to parade around in sweats and an oversized hoodie, still haunted his thoughts every now and then.

If what she said was true, she was in a lot of trouble. He tried to picture the man he spoke to, trying to create a description he could give to the sheriff when he came to speak with Jess. The pursuer had worn a black ball cap and sunglasses, and a blue medical mask had covered his nose and mouth.

He tried to remember other details about the suspect that might help track him down but couldn't think of anything of value. This was also his ex-girlfriend, who he thought he was going to spend his life with. Working for the Oakwood Springs Police Department was supposed to be easy. Not much happens in a small town, but nothing's easy these days.

Jess shivered, leaning closer to him as they walked. He didn't want to imagine what she might have experienced. She had always been the goody-two-shoes type who believed everyone had a good side to them. That illusion had likely just been shattered. As they reached his cabin, Michael glanced over his shoulder, just in case their masked friend was following them. When scanning their surroundings showed nothing, he pushed Jess inside. As he closed the front door, his phone vibrated in his pocket, and he placed it to his ear.

"Well, she was right. There *is* a young woman here. Looks like this has turned from a rescue to a murder investigation," Sheriff Thomas Cook said grimly.

Michael's stomach twisted. He'd dealt with murder many times but had never gotten used to telling people that a friend or loved one had been killed.

He turned to see Jess staring at him. Her eyes pleaded for news that the girl was alright. He exhaled.

Tears rolled down her face as her expression changed from fright to despair. "She's dead, isn't she?"

Michael nodded.

CHAPTER 2

Jess wrapped her arms tightly around herself. She felt like she was a cube of ice that had just been thrown into the fire. Cold sweat dripped from her forehead as she thought about how close she had come to death today. It was all she could do not to completely freak out and fall apart right in front of...him.

Michael Redman. The guy who dumped her in college for her best friend. When she'd found out that he was engaged to Tiffany just a few months after their breakup, she felt as if he'd lied to her their entire relationship, and he was just waiting for a way out so he could be with Tiffany.

She glanced at him out of the corner of her eye. She always used to tell him how perfect he was. His thick black hair and chiseled jaw. Obviously too perfect for her. His piercing blue eyes used to give her butterflies. He knew how to look right into her soul. Maybe that was why it was so easy for him to walk away because she was an obstacle he'd conquered. At least it seemed easy. She'd given her whole heart to him, and he destroyed it. She wasn't about to trust him with anything of hers now.

She drew in a deep breath, eyeing everything in the ranch-style cabin. It had that rustic look that one would expect from a bachelor. By the door, a hat rack held a few camo hats and a policeman's hat that looked similar to the one her friend Tom usually wore.

"When did you move here? Where's Tiffany?" she asked.

Michael's expression seemed to show pain when she mentioned Tiffany. Strange.

"I moved here about six months ago. When the divorce was finalized." Michael gave her a pointed, icy look.

Okay, that's clearly still an open wound. She wanted to tell him it served him right after the way he'd treated her. But she didn't. She'd nearly ended up on the floor next to Annabelle. She would've revealed how vulnerable she felt right now and that her wounds were still open as well.

"Jess, can you tell me what happened?" he asked slowly.

It made her feel like she was in a psych ward all of a sudden. She had no idea why. She'd seen many women in this position hundreds of times. She knew the drill by heart. She must have looked just as weak and fragile. She stiffened up, trying to look brave, searching for the right words.

The police would need any detail she could offer. Even the smallest detail could be used to catch him. She knew all too well the steps that were taken to bring a perpetrator to justice for the women of the community. But this was different. The woman she was trying to save was dead. She'd watched her draw her last breath, and there was nothing she could do about it.

Jess inhaled deeply, then released it, hoping it would help her voice become less shaky. "I went to the house for a home check of one of our girls."

"Your girls?"

"Yes, Annabelle was a victim of domestic violence, and her husband wasn't progressing in his anger management classes very well. We'd heard that she'd moved back in with him before the courts okayed it. At least that's what her file said. Then I found her." Jess felt the terror rebuilding in her chest.

Telling the story to Michael felt as if she was reliving every agonizing second. She'd heard some of the young women she'd helped say the same thing when she would ask them to tell their stories to the police. She'd never really understood what they meant until now.

Hot tears stung her cheeks as she remembered what Annabelle's clothes felt like under her hands. The sight of Annabelle lying on the floor was burned in her mind, and it would never go away.

"Did you know her very well?" Michael asked.

Jess fought back tears. "Not really. I think I've seen her a couple of times at the Safe Haven Group Home, but I took this home check today for someone else."

She couldn't keep the big salty tears from racing down her face and dripping onto her lap. She buried her face in her hands. Mia was about fifteen years older than Jess and had a condition in her knees that wouldn't allow her to move very quickly. If Jess hadn't taken this case for her, she would've likely been lying dead next to Annabelle. All the what-ifs rolled through Jess's mind as she sobbed. She shivered as she began to hyperventilate. Her head throbbed in time with her gasping breaths.

Michael knelt beside her. She did her best not to look at him directly. She could tell he had more questions for her, but before he could ask them, there was a knock at the door. Jess nearly leaped off the couch.

"He's come back! He knows you found me, and—" She jumped up to make a run for it, but her legs felt like jelly.

Michael stood and balled up his fists. He marched toward the door like a tank, ready for battle. It looked like he was going to attack whoever walked through that door.

"Who's there?" he growled.

"Sheriff Tom," a deep voice responded, almost matching the deepness of Michael's.

His fists released as he opened the door. The sheriff stepped inside. The familiar grey hair and weathered face caused relief to wash over her. Jess wanted to give him a huge hug for getting here so quickly. She'd known Sheriff Tom for several years. He'd sort of become her sidekick whenever she was called to the home of one of the many women she helped in the county.

Although Tom would probably say that she was *his* sidekick. It didn't matter to Jess.

He was like a father to her and the first person she called whenever she was in trouble. He'd stepped into that role once he found out that her own father was no longer living. He was her only family since mom died last year. She wished now more than ever before that she had siblings, so the world wouldn't seem like such a lonely place.

"Jessie! Are you alright?" he exclaimed.

"Yes, I'm alright." Her voice shook, making her sound like a liar.

Tom's eyes crinkled with concern. Ever since she moved to Oakwood Springs four years ago, Tom was pretty much the only person who had her back. Due to her dedication to her work, there wasn't much time for friends. Work became a whole lot easier with him around.

He pushed past Michael and plopped on the brown leather couch next to her, wrapping his arm around her. She felt like a child in his embrace. Her body tensed, knowing he was waiting for her to tell him what she saw. She would have to go through it a third time...and would be asked to go over it several more before it was over with.

With another deep breath, she repeated the story she'd told Michael almost word for word as if she had it memorized, pausing a few times during the second telling to take a breath and make her heart slow down.

As she explained what happened, Tom's expression changed. He frowned as if something didn't add up.

"What is it, Tom?" she asked.

His brow furrowed deeper as he rubbed the gray stubble on his chin. "Annabelle Mason. That name seems familiar to me."

"You told me you were called to the scene with Mia just a few months ago," Jess reminded him.

"No. It's something else. Anyway, I'm sure it'll come to me sooner or later. Right now, we need to get you somewhere safe. Since the suspect has your car and your wallet, he pretty much knows your whole life now." Tom explained, crossing his arms.

"I'm not just gonna up and leave town if that's what you're suggesting. I can't leave the girls I care for. They need me," Jess protested.

"And what would they do if you were killed?" Michael added. She glanced over in his direction. He'd been so quiet that she'd almost forgotten he was there. His knee was propped against the arm of the couch near her hand.

"I really think I can be of more help. My job is to help people out of bad situations. I should be able to help myself out of one," she snapped back.

Michael folded his arms. What gave him the idea that he had any say in what she did? He'd removed himself from her life years ago.

"It would be best for your safety if you left town for a few days," Tom's tone told her he wasn't going to allow her to argue with him, but she wasn't going to back down. She'd dealt with rough husbands and boyfriends of the girls in her care before. She wasn't about to let one ruin her life.
*****

Michael had no idea the sheriff knew his ex—the girl he considered the one that got away, in spite of him being the one responsible for their breakup. It had been the most difficult part of his life—a part he'd strived to forget. And he thought he had until she climbed out from under that bush and grabbed his hand.

Her touch caused everything he'd buried in the back of his mind to resurface. He'd allowed the happy memories to reveal themselves every now and then when he,

Jess, and their friend Tiffany were inseparable. Right up until the end.

He distinctly remembered kissing Jess goodbye right before she climbed onto the bus that was heading South, taking her back to her hometown. There weren't many times when she went home to visit her family that he didn't go along with her. But she'd insisted this was different.

After she left, Tiffany told him Jess wasn't going on a family vacation like she said. She was actually seeing someone back home behind his back.

He'd never been as angry as he was that day. Not before or since. He'd called Jess and ended their relationship, not giving her a single second to explain the accusation or defend herself. The only reason he believed that story was because he trusted Tiffany, which turned out to be the biggest mistake of his life.

The memory of why he and Tiffany got married was foggy. Before he knew it, he was a husband and now divorced. But he was okay. He was a survivor. He'd moved on with his life, and Jess was all but forgotten until today.

"I'm not going anywhere." Jess protested, pulling Michael back into reality.

Tom's suggestion that she leave town seemed to genuinely offend her.

"I've dealt with abusive people before. If I run, then I might as well quit my job."

"Jessie, we aren't talking about abuse. We're talking about murder." Tom corrected her.

Jess stared at the floor. Michael could almost see the wheels turning in her head. This was how she processed things. She bit her upper lip and began wringing her hands. He couldn't stand to see her like that.

"How about some coffee, guys?" Michael bolted for the kitchen before they could give an answer. Clenching his jaw, he started the coffee pot and pulled three of his best mugs out of the cabinet.

Tom continued to try to persuade Jess to leave town until this guy was caught.

Jess looked terrified, but Michael knew she was trying to wear her tough face, which didn't look very tough at all. He drew in a deep breath, trying to fight the feelings that were trying hard to come back. The feelings to protect her. The feelings to try and make her smile because he couldn't bear to see her so upset.

But something seemed different. The look Jess wore had a hint of guilt in it.

Michael frowned, remembering what signs to look for during an interrogation that suggested guilt. He didn't want to think of her that way, but his instincts tugged at the corner of his mind. There was no way she could be involved, could there be? No, he shoved those thoughts out of his head. The Jess he knew couldn't hurt a fly.

During their freshman year, he remembered taking her to the movies, and when they came out, there was a daddy-long-legs perched on his car. He wanted to kill it, but she picked it up and sent it on its way. That was who she was.

A few moments later, he carried two cups of coffee into the living room and placed them on the antique tea table in front of Tom and Jess. He recalled his mother telling him that the table would go with a masculine or feminine decor when she gave it to him as a wedding present. He cringed at the memory. He could ask himself why for the billionth time, but it wouldn't help anything. *What's done is done.* And there wasn't anything he could say or do that would change it.

Marrying someone he didn't love was something he always said he'd never do. He knew he didn't really love Tiffany, not the way he'd loved Jess. Holding the truth inside of himself, saying "I do" while looking in Tiffany's eyes, had made him feel hollow, but he hadn't felt like himself in years. He pulled a small armchair up to the table, propping his elbows on his knees.

Michael never thought he would be this close to Jess ever again. He'd thought time and time again about what he would say if he ever ran into her. He'd even considered trying to find her to tell her how sorry he was. Now that she was sitting here, right in front of him, all those words and apologies were nowhere to be found. He watched her for a moment, trying to think of something he could say that would help the situation. Her eyes squeezed shut, and Tom patted her shoulder to comfort her.

Michael wanted to think of something he could do to help. Anything. Then he got an idea. An idea he knew Jess wouldn't care for at all, but she didn't have a lot of options. A small voice in the back of his mind told him that what he was about to propose, he would probably regret.

"Here's a crazy idea," Michael said before he could stop himself. "What if you stayed here for a few days?"

Both pairs of eyes stared at him for a moment. The regret slowly crept into his chest. *That was quick.*

"Not in a million years. I have a friend in Cincinnati who I can stay with. I have a week of vacation time. I don't need your charity or your help," Jess frowned at him. She seemed disgusted at the thought.

Ouch! Michael bit the inside of his cheek so he wouldn't fire a quip back at her. He definitely regretted his suggestion.

"Fine, I'll take you there myself," Tom chimed in.

Michael thought it best to keep his mouth shut moving forward.

CHAPTER 3

Jess adjusted herself in the front seat of Tom's police cruiser. Her stomach grumbled. She'd missed having anything for lunch because of this whole ordeal. Guilt overcame her. How could she think about food right now?

An unwelcome image of Annabelle's lifeless body lying on the floor flashed in her mind. Annabelle was dead now because of her. If Jess had gotten there a few minutes earlier, maybe she would still be alive. Deep down, she knew that wasn't the truth. Judging from the amount of blood surrounding her body, it was too late to save her. Every detail seemed permanently etched in her mind. Her face and red hair. A face she recognized.

"Ready to go?" Tom climbed into the driver's seat.

Jess shrugged. She was "ready" to crawl into bed and cry until there wasn't an ounce of fluid left in her body. Annabelle deserved that much. There was no doubt that this was the same Annabelle she'd met when she was twelve. Growing up an only child had been difficult, but when she heard that a family with children had moved in next door, the thought of having someone to play with was much more than exciting.

The family had a girl about her age and two smaller children. She and Annabelle became fast friends, and the two were inseparable for about a year. But one day, Annabelle wasn't able to come over anymore. Mom said that Annabelle's mother had abandoned their family. It was beyond her how any mother could leave their family like that.

But Annabelle snuck into her house one night and told Jess she was running away to go find her mother. Jess told on her.

She remembered the words she said to the thirteen-year-old version of the girl she tried to save today. "Your father needs you, and you want to leave him too."

"You don't understand. He's mean to me," Annabelle pleaded.

The last thing she remembered of Annabelle was her face peering out the back window of their station wagon between the piles of their belongings. It wasn't until a few weeks later that they learned how Annabelle's mother was actually missing after she filed a complaint against her husband for domestic violence. He'd beaten her and Annabelle both.

Tears rolled down Jess's face as the last image of thirteen-year-old Annabelle filled her mind. She wasn't there for her then, and she certainly hadn't been there for her today.

Jess stared out the car window, pondering the misdeeds of her childhood as the wooded area turned into suburbs. It took her a while to get used to small-town life but moving here gave her the fresh start she wanted after things ended between her and Michael. Now he was here... and had been here for a little while. How had she not seen him or bumped into him at all in the last six months? Did he know she was here and just avoided her all this time?

Surely, she would've bumped into him sooner or later. His bright smile and jokester personally made him popular quicker than the average person. It was what attracted her to him from the start. No. She wasn't going to dwell on him right now. She quickly pushed Michael out of her mind.

The smell of black coffee and leather permeated Tom's car. She felt the tightness in her chest loosen, grateful to have someone like him in her life—someone she could call on, night or day.

He'd been the officer to respond to the very first removal she had to do. She will never forget how nervous she felt that day. The young woman she was there to help called the Crisis Center and said she wanted to get away from her boyfriend, but she didn't want him to go to jail. Jess had to call the police when she saw the bruises and bloodstains on the girl's face. After taking the girl to the hospital, she and Tom went out for coffee. That was their custom to this day.

"Another life saved," Tom would say.

They'd saved more than fifty lives since that day. Now they were trying to save her own.

"You know, this is the first girl I've lost." Jess focused on the scuff marks etched into the dash.

"That girl dying wasn't your fault, Jessie. They told me there wasn't anything that could be done by the time you got to her. The knife hit one of her arteries. You wouldn't have been able to stop the bleeding. No matter how hard you tried," Tom softly responded. He reached over and gave her shoulder a pat.

Jess should've been able to take some kind of solace in that, but she didn't. She couldn't. She'd failed Annabelle before, and now she had again. The guilt she'd carried all these years had doubled.

"I can't help but feel like there was something else I could've done to save her," Jess whispered.

"Maybe it's best not to think about it right now. Tell me about this friend I'm taking you to."

Tom's attempt to change the subject was a little too straightforward, but she was willing to give it a try.

"Tammy is your typical girly girl with a passion for helping children," Jess began.

Telling him the quick story of how she met Tammy seemed to brighten the car a little bit. She became friends with Tammy not long after her breakup with Michael. She was also a Social Work major at Mountainview University but had to drop out after the loss of her sister.

"So she's alright with you staying with her?" Tom asked.

"Yeah. She seemed happy that I'm coming," Jess pulled at the shoulder strap of her seat belt. She'd never been so fidgety. She was going to be alright at Tammy's.

"She thought I needed to stay with her because of a guy," Jess added. She could always count on Tammy to ask probing questions.

"Well, you kind of are. But you didn't tell her what was going on. Right? I mean, the less she knows, the better."

"No, I didn't tell her why I'm coming. I just told her I'm coming for a visit for a week." Jess leaned against the backrest, taking deep breaths in hopes of relaxing a bit before they reached Cincinnati. She wanted to make the best of this situation and enjoy her time with Tammy.

I WILL find her.

The killer's words echoed in her mind. She sat back up in the seat. Her heart pounded as she remembered his promise. Maybe it wasn't such a good idea to go to Tammy's. What if they were followed? Jess looked over her shoulder out the back window of the police cruiser. She didn't see any suspicious looking cars behind them. She had to get a grip.

This would be over before she knew it. But what if it wasn't? No, she couldn't think like that. Jess's stomach ached.

"What's this business with you and Michael Redman?" Tom asked. She let out an exaggerated sigh. It would be best if they stayed as far away from that topic as possible.

"We used to date in college." Giving Tom the short answer was the easy route, but with another hour and a half of driving ahead of them, she knew that wouldn't be the end of it.

"I knew that by the way you two looked at each other. I want to know what happened," he added.

"My best friend told him I was seeing someone behind his back. I wasn't. Then he broke up with me. I found out a year later that they were married. In a blink, I lost two people who I thought would be in my life forever." Jess had no idea why she was telling Tom as much as she was.

She thought of Tom as a good friend, but her problems were hers, and she hated revealing how emotionally broken she felt. She worked at a Crisis Center. She was supposed to be the one that had it all together.

"I think you should talk it out with him. You obviously still have feelings for him."

"I do not. I haven't seen him in years, and I want nothing to do with him."

That was true, up until this morning when he wrapped his arm around her and led her into his house. She'd often missed how safe he made her feel. How loved she felt. But that was over, and she wasn't about to place her heart on the chopping block again for him to destroy.

"Michael has only been a deputy for about six months, but I can tell he's a good guy." Tom had his wrists crossed over the top of the steering wheel, slightly moving them back and forth.

"Well, you don't know him like I do," Jess replied.

"How long ago did you break up?"

"It's been about six years now." Had it really been that long? The amount of hurt she still carried from it made it seem like it had only been a few months.

"You know, people can change a lot in six years." It was becoming clear that Tom would press this conversation to a point she didn't want to go to.

"Yes, and some people never change." She crossed her arms.

Tom gave her a sideways glance and held up a hand in surrender. "Alright, message received.".

*****

Michael looked at his couch where Jess had been sitting just a little while ago. He'd imagined her sitting there so many times that he had to question if today had been a dream or if she'd really been here. He grabbed his coat and walked out to his pickup truck. Spring was beginning to settle in, but the winter chill still hovered in the air when the sun set. It would be about a month or so before he would be able to leave his jacket at home, but that was typical in Oakwood Springs, Ohio. That was one of the things he loved about it, though. One was able to fully experience every season at its finest.

It would've been an average day for him if Jess hadn't stumbled back into his life. How could he not know she lived here? She'd been here the entire time. He could've passed her on his way to work. He could've been in the same grocery store with her. The thought of that bothered him more than anything. She was so close, yet so far away. Of all the small towns in the world to move to, why did he have to come here? The chances were a billion to one.

As pine trees and perennials sprouting lime green buds flew past his window, Michael let his complicated situation with Jess fade to the back of his mind. What was more important right now was why he ran into her in the woods in the first place. He knew the house she'd come from. They were his closest neighbors, but he didn't know anything about them. He wasn't thrilled by the fact that a murder had taken place so close to his home, but he was grateful he was able to save Jess from a horrible fate.

He would've offered to take her where she needed to go if Tom hadn't told him to go to the scene of the crime to make sure there weren't any further clues.

As Michael turned into the small cul-de-sac driveway, he noticed the tech team had already left, but there was still a police car parked in front of the house. He stopped his truck only a few feet from where the steep porch steps met the ground. The stairs were a light oak color that hadn't been stained yet. They must've been built recently.

Michael scanned the ground surrounding the steps to see if maybe Jess had dropped something as she was escaping. As he looked, the sound of footsteps on the porch caused him to reach for the gun he had tucked in the back of his jeans. He looked up to see a figure stepping out the front door. It was Harry, his closest friend.

"Isn't this your day off?" The deputy called to him as he started up the steps to meet him.

"Crime never takes a day off, Harold. What can I say?" Michael replied.

The young deputy frowned at him. "It's Harry, and you know that." He said, pointing at him with a long blue rubber-gloved finger. Harry Miller was a few years younger than Michael, but he was likable and reminded him of his younger brother Kyle.

"Tom told me to come and help you look for clues that might lead us to the perp." Michael passed Harry on the porch as he entered the front room.

Harry turned and followed him.

Michael stood in the living room for a moment, taking in every detail. The dark red walls gave the room an eerie feeling, almost like something out of an Edgar Allen Poe story. Michael couldn't help but dread investigating a murder scene. He loved his job but seeing a dead body being carted away turned his stomach. Not to mention the feeling of loss that hovered in the air. The loss of life. He'd dealt with some evil people, the kind whose eyes were full of darkness and death.

"Why would someone paint their walls red?" Harry asked, keeping at his heels.

"My mom's kitchen walls are red," Michael commented.

"No. Like burgundy or an apple red is okay, but this is like vampire blood red. It makes this tiny room seem even smaller," Harry said.

Michael nodded in agreement. He could tell by the nervous tick in Harry's voice that he was slowly getting creeped out.

"Some abuse victims prefer smaller spaces because it makes them feel safer. Also, some abusers want their victims to feel alone and secluded to form an emotional dependency." Michael was reciting something he'd heard his psychology professor say.

"Or whoever lived here liked the Twilight series on an unhealthy level."

Michael rolled his eyes at Harry's joke.

Harry started flipping on every light he came across as they made their way through the house. The now lit-up room revealed some pictures of the victim and her husband. Two small couches, an end table, and an armchair next to the doorway that led into the kitchen.

Some photos of the couple had been professionally taken, while others showed them standing in front of tourist sights all over the country.

Michael reached behind him, waving his hand in Harry's direction. "Give me a glove."

Harry handed him a blue rubber glove. Michael pulled it on with a snap and picked up a small wooden frame. The couple was standing by a viewpoint that seemed to be overlooking the Grand Canyon. Annabelle wore a forced half smile while her husband, a short stocky guy with reddish blonde hair, had an arm over her shoulder. Judging from the angle of his arm, Michael assessed that he had to be standing on his tiptoes to achieve the pose.

"He looks like the poster child for a Napoleon complex if you ask me," Harry quipped.

"People come in all shapes and sizes, Harry." Michael didn't really like to pass judgment on people but had to admit that the guy did fit the profile for being abusive.

"Have we brought him in for questioning?" Michael wiped a gloved finger down the edge of the frame, revealing a sticky red substance that was almost completely dry.

"We are still trying to find him," Harry responded.

"We determined which room the murder took place in, right?" Michael asked.

"Yes, the forensic team said her carotid artery was cut with one blow, and the victim died in minutes. So where she was found in the kitchen was where she was stabbed," Harry confirmed.

Michael chewed on the inside of his cheek as he weighed the facts in his mind. So that would mean the victim was stabbed just as Jess was walking through the door. That had to catch the murderer off guard.

"If you ask me, I think the killer has background experience in the medical field. Who else would know exactly where to stab someone that would kill them almost instantly?" Harry circled the living room, scanning the walls.

"Not a bad theory." Michael placed the framed picture back down where he found it.

"Check into the background of the husband for me. Figure out where he was, what he does for a living, and when was the last time he saw his wife." Michael ordered.

"Well, we already know that his name is Linus Mason, and he works at the lumber mill on Knox Road. Due to the domestic violence charges against him, he was staying with his parents until he completed his anger management classes."

Michael gave him a nod of approval. "Nice job."

As he walked into the kitchen, the room opened to reveal a back door just to the right of where he was standing. The kitchen was a little brighter than the living room and had bigger windows. Michael let his eyes take in every single detail. From the white curtains with roosters on them to the black and white checkerboard flooring and the large red stain next to the sink. The gray countertop held more rooster figurines, a small bowl of fruit, and a collection of kitchen knives.

Michael gently stepped through, making sure he didn't let his shoes touch the red stain. He looked over the knives. None of them were missing. He turned to see Harry still standing in the living room, taking notes on everything Michael asked him to do.

Out of the corner of his eye, he saw a shadow move across the wall. Someone was watching them from just outside the back door.

CHAPTER 4

Michael darted for the door the moment his eyes recognized the undeniable shape of a person.

"*Stop, police!*" Michael yelled, darting off after the figure. He threw the door open and caught sight of a bright blue shirt, jeans, and black sneakers disappearing into the trees.

The chill of the spring evening and the breeze from his run caused his lungs to immediately burn and his eyes to water. The setting sun brought more shadows to the woods, making it easier for someone to hide. Michael panted, pushing himself to run faster. He squinted, making sure he kept focus. He wasn't about to let whoever this was get away.

Michael leaped over a fallen tree and followed the trail around a bend. He could still hear the crunching of the fallen leaves from last winter with each step he took. His footsteps seemed to echo between the trees. No, that was the footsteps of whoever he was chasing. He was getting closer. He could see a flash of blue in the distance as the person whipped around a massive bushy pine tree. Due to the thickness of the tree branches and bushes, it was hard to see if it was a man or a woman.

Please don't let me lose him, he prayed. Michael's lips formed a circle, keeping his breaths deep so he wouldn't run out of steam. He clenched his jaw, pushing himself on. Now was not a good time to think about whether he was a bad person or not. Whoever was in the blue jacket had led him to a trail that seemed to be very worn. The path bowed into a tiny ravine, letting Michael know exactly where they were headed.

After about four miles, this trail would bring them to the outskirts of town. Michael came to a stop, taking a few seconds to think. He wasn't going to catch him this way. He would have to cut around the path through the thick grove of trees and head him off. He turned and took a different trail that took him back toward his house.

Something disturbing occurred to him as he began running toward where he figured the blue jacketed figure would come out. If his calculations were correct, this would be the trail Jess was on this afternoon while she was running for her life. The idea of Jess running from a maniac sent rage through him. He couldn't imagine who would want to kill her. Even though she didn't have anything nice to say to him earlier, she was the nicest person he'd ever met and would go above and beyond to help anyone. The anger he felt and the thought that this person was potentially involved fueled him, pushing him forward.

Michael came to where the trail forked off, and he was sure he'd made his way around the thicker part of the woods, which would slow anyone who tried to get through way down, allowing him to get in front of them. Only a few seconds had passed when Michael heard the rustling of leaves and cracking of branches just a few yards away from him. As if on cue, the blue jacket came into view, and Michael chased after him.

As he got closer, he noticed whoever this was didn't have the same build as the man he'd encountered before Jess's appearance. His heart sank a little. This wasn't the killer, nor the man who said he would find Jess. Still, they could have crucial information. Maybe they saw something. They wouldn't be running if they didn't have anything to hide.

Michael heard a wheezing sound growing louder. As he came to the clearing, he saw the blue figure bend over with his hands on his knees. His body heaved, gasping for air. He was either horribly out of shape or asthmatic. The closer he got, the more he was able to determine that this was the victim's husband. He remembered the small framed reddish blonde hair from the photo.

"Alright, alright. You got me," Linus Mason squeaked out between wheezes.

Michael tried to hide the fact that he was also trying to catch his breath. He was a bit out of shape as well, but he wasn't having near as much trouble as Linus was. What should he do? He'd never dealt with an asthmatic before. After a few minutes, Linus seemed to be breathing normally. So, he thought it best to ignore it.

"Mr. Mason, did you know that running from the cops is always a bad idea?" Michael grabbed him by the arms and pulled them behind his back. "You're coming with me. You have the right to remain silent,"

Michael gritted his teeth as he quoted the rest of the Miranda rights. He pulled a pair of handcuffs from the pocket of his jeans and slapped them on Linus's wrists. He mentally gave himself Kudos for remembering to grab them out of his truck when he got to the murder site.

"I haven't done anything illegal." Linus jerked his arm, trying to pull his small hand through the cuffs. He nearly knocked himself and Michael over with all the tugging and pulling.

Michael took the extra precaution to squeeze the cuffs tighter on his wrists. Linus Mason may not be the killer, but that didn't mean he should underestimate him.

"Then why did you run?" Michael asked.

"I see police cars parked in front of my house, and you think I'm just gonna walk right up and say hello?" Linus gave a firm and quick pull, freeing his jacket from Michael's grasp, and bolted.

"Oh no, you don't." Michael sprinted a few steps as well and grabbed another handful of his jacket with a tighter squeeze.

"I didn't do anything wrong," Linus objected once again.

"Maybe not, but I need to ask you some questions. You're coming down to the station," Michael ushered him back to the trailer.

As they emerged from the woods, Harry stood waiting for him near the car. He opened the back of his police cruiser, allowing Michael to shove him inside.

"Maybe you'd better go home and change. You'd get in less trouble if you were wearing your uniform," Harry advised.

Michael looked down at his clothes. He'd forgotten he was in his jeans and boots. "Yeah, maybe you're right. Give me about an hour, and I'll meet you at the station."

*****

Jess pulled her phone from her pocket. She tapped the screen, gritting her teeth when it remained black. Tom slammed the car door behind him. They were trying to get to Cincinnati before it got late. But that wasn't going to happen now because of the flat tire Tom had just finished fixing. "My phone is dead. Can I borrow yours to let Tammy know we'll be late?"

Tom handed her his flip phone.

"You're still using this? You've had this same phone since I've known you," she poked.

"And a long while before that." He smirked back at her.

He was a good sport, and she couldn't help but tease him every now and then for being set in his ways. She rolled her eyes and placed the flip phone against her cheek, waiting for Tammy to answer. The clock on Tom's dashboard read 9:45. Fifteen minutes later than Jess said they would be arriving at her house, and they were still thirty minutes out. She owed Tammy a huge apology.

No answer. That was odd. Jess tried Tammy's cell phone again. Nothing. A flicker of anxiety hit the pit of her stomach. It wasn't like Tammy not to answer her phone.

No, Tammy is okay. Jess took a slow, deep breath as she tried to reassure herself.

There was nothing in her house that would indicate Tammy's as the first place she would go in an emergency. Even if the killer completely ransacked her tiny house. There would be very little evidence that she even knew Tammy. Maybe a picture here and there. Nothing with her address or even her name. That thought gave Jess a little peace of mind, but not much.

"Is she not answering?" Tom glanced at her.

Her face must have worn a look of worry for him to ask.

"No. She's probably stuck in front of the TV." Her attempt to sound nonchalant about it was a bad one. Tom obviously saw through it by the way his expression sobered.

"All the same, I'd like to get there as soon as possible. I fixed the flat as quickly as I could. We don't need to be caught sitting out in the open like that. Thank God it was dark." As Tom took the exit, Jess got a quick view of the Cincinnati skyline in the distance. Maybe when this was over, she could come up here and see what made this city so special.

As they turned onto Tammy's street, her house came into view. Alarm flared up Jess's spine. Tammy's house was totally dark, as if she hadn't been there all day. She expected to see at least one light somewhere in the house. Jess shot a look at Tom, who also looked concerned. He stopped the car directly in front of the house and got out.

"Stay here and lock the doors," he ordered before hurrying up the porch steps.

She peered out the window after Tom, her face so close to the window that she had to wipe the fog away each time she exhaled. Tom's dark silhouette knocked on the front door. She could make out a hand on his hip just in case he needed to draw his pistol.

After knocking a few times, Tom tried the door. Jess watched his form disappear into the house. Another red flag. Tammy never left her door unlocked. Something was really wrong. After he was inside for a few seconds, a light turned on in the living room. Her heart caught in her throat.

God, please let Tammy be alright. She waited for what seemed like years before Tom came rushing back out of the house.

Jess rolled down her window. "What's going on?"

"Call an ambulance! Your friend has been attacked." Tom barked.

"What! No. No. No." Jess pushed the car door open and leaped out.

He grabbed her arm. "Don't go in there, Jessie."

"That's my friend. Oh, this is all my fault." Jess burst into tears.

Tom grabbed his phone from the car and called the local police. She could hear him giving them the details of the scene to the Cincinnati P.D. as he followed her into the house. The sight of Tammy's limp form sprawled out on the living room floor felt like another punch to the gut.

"Tammy!" She dropped to her friend's side and turned her body over.

Her skin was still warm. That gave Jess some hope. Tammy's light pink shirt had a dark stain on the shoulder, indicating that she had been stabbed just like Annabelle had. How could the killer beat her and Tom here? She knew since he had her car that he had her house keys. He also had her purse and her wallet, giving him access to her money and checkbook. Which meant he had access to her bank account information too. The killer had access to every part of her life.

Jess grabbed the tablecloth from an end table that had been knocked over, pressing it to Tammy's shoulder in an attempt to stop the bleeding. Tammy moaned. That was when Jess noticed she also had a large bump on her forehead near her hairline.

Whoever had done this to Tammy wasn't trying to kill her. If they were, they would have. They came here for a specific reason. They had probably used the same knife she'd seen clutched in his hand just this afternoon. She was angry with herself for getting Tammy involved with her problems. But how did he know this was the first place she'd come?

She couldn't hold back the sobs.

God has great things in store for you. Her mother's words echoed through her mind. All her life, she had trouble believing it....... but now. What could God possibly have in store for her if it meant she was going to be hunted by a killer? Although she knew it was wrong, she was angry with God for allowing this to happen.

Tom knelt next to Jess. "The ambulance is here."

Two paramedics lifted Tammy from her arms, placing her on a clean white gurney.

As she watched them cart her friend out the door, she turned to Tom. "I'm going to the hospital with her."

"I don't think that's a good idea. At least not right now. If the killer knew you were coming here and somehow managed to beat us here, he'll figure you'll follow her to the hospital. We can't take that risk."

Tom was right. But her own safety didn't matter right now. She had to know that Tammy was going to be okay.

"You're probably right about that. But I can't just leave her alone. I'm going." Jess clenched her jaw.

Tom huffed. "Alright, but you're not riding in the ambulance."

62

CHAPTER 5

Jess sat by Tammy's hospital bed, rolling the events of the day over in her mind. She never would've guessed things would play out like this when she'd first gotten out of bed this morning. The cold gray room of the hospital seemed to be getting smaller with each beep of the monitor.

She wouldn't be one hundred percent safe anywhere, but she didn't have a "safe" job to start with. Countless times she'd been standing beside her car with a terrified young woman in the back seat. She didn't have a problem guarding the door with an angry husband or boyfriend threatening her. She wasn't afraid then. Tom always showed up on time and carted them off, giving Jess time to get the frightened women to safety.

But this wasn't a job. This was one of her dearest friends. Lying in a coma right in front of her. And it was her fault.

"Please pull through this," she whispered.

People in comas could hear you talking to them. That was true, wasn't it? She'd heard that somewhere and prayed it was. Tears trickled down her cheeks just as the doorknob clicked. Panic filled her chest. She whirled around—Tom's warning that the killer would expect her to be here echoing in her head. She would have to fight to the death. She balled her fists, ready to execute a punch to the nose to whoever stepped through that door.

The door slowly opened, and Michael's face peeked around it. "Hey, I got here as soon as I could," he whispered.

He entered the room with another man who looked to be a little bit older than Michael. "This is a friend of mine, Detective Carl Simpson of the Cincinnati PD."

The Detective stuck his hand out. Jess reluctantly grabbed it, letting the detective give it a firm shake.

"Michael tells me that you know the victim." Carl began, pulling a small notepad and pencil from his pocket.

"Yes, she's one of my closest friends," Jess said tearfully.

"Michael also told me about the incident this afternoon. We can't say for sure right now that the two attacks are related until we gather all the evidence."

"I understand," Jess muttered.

"Is there anything else you can tell us about the victim that might lead us to who did this? Maybe an ex or something," Carl asked.

Jess thought for a moment. Tammy hadn't dated anyone for a long time. She hadn't even spoken to her ex in two years, and they ended things on relatively good terms. She tried to think of anything the police could use that might help them link what happened to her and what happened to Tammy. The two had to be related. It was too much of a coincidence.

"I can't think of anything," she finally answered.

"We'll have an officer here at all times to protect Ms. Lenore and that we're doing everything we can to catch whoever did this." Carl handed her a small white card.

"If you can think of anything, please don't hesitate to give me a call."

He turned his attention to Michael. Jess didn't hear any of the conversation between the two. Her attention fell back on the motionless body of her friend. About thirty seconds later, she heard the door close.

She glanced over her shoulder to see if she was alone with Tammy. Alone. That was a word she was all too familiar with. Growing up, her parents worked most of the time. They told her they loved her often, but she still felt like she had no one. Her dolls and stuffed animals were the only ones she could talk to about how she felt.

It wasn't much different in her teen years. Her parents felt less and less obligated to come home and check on her. They loved being able to travel the world. She'd never seen any two people more in love. Maybe they were so in love they forgot to put some aside for her. She felt like one of their many possessions—something to show off once in a while but kept on a shelf in the corner.

She thought the loneliness was gone for good when she met Tiffany and Michael, but she ended up right back where she started, or at least she thought. But then she met Tammy. Tammy had been the one person in her life that has remained a true friend, and now, she was lying here fighting for her life.

Please, God. Would He perform a miracle for someone who was angry with him? Tears formed in her eyes, but she wiped them away before they could wet her cheeks.

"You want me to get you anything?" Michael's voice said from behind her. She jumped.

"Never sneak up on me like that!" She growled, her hands trembling.

She turned to face him. He stood near the door with his hands shoved in his pockets. He raised his shoulders as he responded

"Sorry," he muttered. She could tell he was having trouble knowing what to say. He was the last person she wanted there to comfort her, but at least she wasn't totally alone. But the fact that he was the one person who'd broken her trust more than her parents... Maybe being totally alone wasn't so bad. She raised her chin to look him in the eye and tell him to go away, but her gaze locked onto his instead.

His blue eyes used to be the one place she found peace and reassurance. Now, she expected to see pity or sympathy—as if she'd gotten herself into a mess, like some animal about to become a predator's next meal, but he stepped in and freed her from a trap before she was gobbled up. It was hard to hide her feelings from Michael. He knew her too well, or at least he knew the old her. The vulnerable doe-eyed girl who fell hard for him.

She searched Michael's face, spotting something that aggravated her even more than pity. Did he feel the same way she did? Like he was just as heartbroken over the situation as she was. If only they could be the old Jess and the old Michael for a little bit, so she could feel that safe, comforting feeling again. She looked away, breaking any kind of connection that could form between them.

As if reading her mind, Michael started toward her, wrapping her tightly in his arms. Jess buried her face in his chest, letting herself cry freely. This time, she cried because she wanted to. There was no point in trying to be strong in front of him any longer. It was a façade, and she no longer had the strength to keep up. Hopelessness crept inside of her. If the killer was going to these measures, it would only be a matter of time before...

"He's gonna find me and kill me. I should've never come here. I led him right to her," she sobbed.

Michael took a step back, forcing her to look up at him. "This isn't your fault. Things happen that are out of our control.

You can either fight back or let it win. You've got a pretty strong team on your side."

The sobs and sniffles forced her to breathe in his sandalwood cologne. The familiar scent helped her calm down after a few minutes. He would fight with her? That was reassuring...and dangerous.

A familiar feeling swept over her. The very same feeling she would get when they were walking home after date night. Michael would wrap a protective arm around her shoulder, shielding her from the darkness. She'd missed that so many times over the years. The feeling of being completely safe and not having to fend for herself when she was frightened. She missed him.

"Thanks." She sniffled, pulling away from his grip.

"No problem. If it makes you feel any better, I called in a favor with Carl to make sure he was on this case. He's the best of the best."

His confidence in his friend was reassuring.

"Jess, I know things ended badly between us, but I just wanna—"

She held up her hand and stopped him. That was the very direction she did *not* want to go. The past was the past, and she wasn't about to risk her already broken heart by going back.

"It's alright. It was a long time ago. It's not important now."

This wasn't the time or the place to dig into old wounds. A friendly face to comfort her was the thing she really needed, not the fluttering in her stomach she got every time she looked at him.

He'd changed into his policeman uniform. Tom must've called him and told him what had happened to Tammy. His icy blue eyes had gotten a shade darker since she'd last seen him as if the events of the day troubled him just as badly as they did her.

"But. I..." Michael ran his long fingers through his jet black hair. He always did that when he was nervous.

There was once a time she found it adorable. She was annoyed with herself because, for some reason, she still found it adorable.

How could he think trying to mutter an apology after all these years would make her forgive him? As if there was no harm done. He probably felt obligated to since protecting her was now part of his job. Being a policeman was something he'd dreamed about since she'd first met him.

Jess decided the best thing to do was change the subject before he made things more awkward than they already were. "I've decided that as soon as I know Tammy is okay, I'm going back to Oakwood Springs."

She clenched her jaw, ready with a response for when he tried to forbid her because it wasn't safe. He would try to argue that it would be better if she went somewhere else where the killer was less likely to look for her. Doing that to start with didn't do her any good. The killer had predicted her next move so precisely that he beat her to the punch.

"I think that's an excellent idea," Michael replied.

Jess's right eyebrow flew up in surprise. "Really? No objections?"

"Nope. Only conditions." His Adam's apple bounced once as he swallowed.

She knew he was about to tell her something she didn't want to hear. Jess raised both her eyebrows, waiting for him to continue.

"You're staying with me. I've already talked it over with Tom, and he thinks it's a good idea too." His arms crossed as he'd finished.

"No one thought to ask me what I think?" Jess objected, bringing her hand to her hip.

"It's for your own safety, and my house is out of the way," Michael shot back.

"I know. Still, someone could've included me in the plans." Jess wanted to protest further, to go home and never see him again. But that wasn't an option right now. She did feel safer with him around and hoped he didn't catch the relief on her face.

"Fine. But since you wanna be a big hero, I wanna go by my apartment and get a few things. I need some clothes and toiletries." She crossed her arms, matching his stance.

She would go along with this until the killer was caught, but Tom was going to get an earful for doing this to her after she explained to him about their past relationship.

"Fine by me. I'll check back in a little while to make sure you're okay. If you hear anything about your friend beforehand, just let one of the officers know, and they'll call me," He used his head to point toward the door.

"Where will you be?" Now she sounded like a frightened child.

"I'm gonna grab a cup of coffee down a few blocks. You want one?" He asked, his features remaining soft toward her.

She nodded.

"Be back soon," He let the door gently close behind him. Why didn't he get upset and annoyed by her protests? Any disagreement between them would keep them distant and strictly professional. She could've let things get to a personal level again, but there was just too much pain between them. Pain she wasn't able to deal with right now. He must've expected her to put up more of a fight than that—which was probably why he went to Tom about it first. He knew she was more likely to listen to Tom.

Jess wished she could talk to him about someone else protecting her during the investigation. She still could and had every right to, but she also knew there probably wasn't anyone as capable of doing the job as well as Michael.

Didn't he realize he was tearing open the wound he'd given her all those years ago? The hurt. The anger. Everything she'd put behind her was all coming back. She wasn't supposed to let him get to her, but he was.

*****

Michael thought it best to leave Jess alone with her friend for a bit while he stepped out for a cup of coffee. His uniform was still damp from where she'd sobbed into his chest. It wasn't a good idea to hug her like that again. He was a deputy sheriff, and she was a witness in a murder investigation.

They weren't together anymore. A mistake he still regretted to this day. Not that he hadn't tried to forget her and move on. He'd been reminded on a regular basis of his mistake every time Tiffany decided to give him a swift kick to the shin with her designer leather boots for no apparent reason.

He'd never forget the humiliation he felt whenever he would walk into work with a limp. Thank God the uniforms at the Cincinnati PD were black pants. He had no idea how he would've explained the big black bruises on his legs. His co-workers would have either laughed at him or called him a coward. It was more difficult hiding bite and claw marks on his arms.

He would often try to wear a long-sleeved athletic shirt under his uniform, hoping no one would call him out on it. He remembered one of the other officers talking about a call that came in about a domestic disturbance. A woman took a golf club to her husband because he'd gotten a phone call from someone who happened to be a woman.

Tiffany was a lot like that. Michael wasn't sure she ever loved him. It wasn't until after their divorce that he found out she had been seeing someone else for a long time. He suspected she made up the story about Jess just to break them up because she couldn't stand how happy they were.

Michael exited the hospital through the front entrance after navigating its complicated twists and turns. The twenty-four-hour coffee shop was just a few blocks away. It was a popular spot for cops working night patrol. He prayed he wouldn't see anyone he knew there. They would ask questions. Awkward, uncomfortable questions he didn't want to answer. Like why he left and where he'd been. Leaving a job as a Cincinnati police officer to become a deputy in a tiny town wasn't exactly a career-building move.

The night air was chilly and burned his lungs a little, but he was happy to be getting some time to think and clear his head. He would need to figure out a way to protect Jess without drumming up old memories. It hurt enough just being close to her and not being able to talk about what went wrong between them.

Michael felt a breeze as the door of the coffee shop opened in front of him. He stopped in his tracks. The two and a half block walk went by faster than he'd realized. If the door hadn't caught his attention, he probably would've kept going for at least a mile or two.

He entered, immediately spotting two officers sitting at a table in the corner. They must be on their break. For a second, it looked like one of them pointed at him. He ordered two lattes, then turned and hurried out the door the second the hot paper cups were handed to him.

Michael quickened his pace back to the hospital. He wanted to get the coffee to Jess before it cooled too much. She loved her lattes piping hot, at least she used to. He hoped she didn't read too much into him bringing her coffee. He figured they both had a long night ahead of them, and they could each use the caffeine boost.

When he got back to the ICU, he noticed there was only one officer remaining outside of the room. Michael was glad he didn't know the guy. Or at least he didn't remember him. He gave the bearded officer a nod and got one in return, indicating that it was alright for him to enter. Good, Tom had let the unknown officer know that he would be coming back. He didn't want to go through the headache of showing his badge and confirming his identity. He was all about taking safety precautions, but the Cincinnati PD was the last place in the world he wanted to be seen.

Jess was sitting in the same place he left her—at Tammy's bedside. She looked over her shoulder when he entered the room, then turned back to face her friend without a word.

He went and stood next to her chair, extending the cup right under her nose so the warm caramel fragrance would catch her attention. "Here's your latte."

As he suspected, Jess's gaze met the cup as if she hadn't noticed it before. She grabbed it and took a sip.

"Mmmm." She gave him a small smile. "Caramel. I can't believe you remembered."

She had no idea just how much he remembered about her. Caramel lattes being her favorite hot beverage, was just one of many.

"How could I forget? Remember that time I brought you hot tea during that study group?" he reminded her.

"Yeah, I had to choke it down because I didn't want to hurt your feelings." They were working on a project for their sociology class. Jess, Tiffany, and another guy, whose name he couldn't recall, were sitting around a table in the student lounge when he walked in with drinks. Tiffany had told him all girls loved hot tea. What she didn't know was that Jess wasn't like other girls.

"I'll never forget the look on your face when you took the first sip." Michael pressed his lips together, holding back a chuckle.

Jess smirked. Then her expression returned to the somber look she had before, and she turned back toward Tammy.

"Who would do something like this?" She buried her face in the palms of her hands.

Michael set his coffee cup down on the table next to Tammy's bed, then gently squeezed her shoulder. "There are a lot of bad people in this world."

He wished he had something more insightful to say. Something that would make her feel better and give her hope.

A short blonde nurse entered the room. Jess stood and watched her expectantly.

She checked Tammy's vitals and all the machines she was hooked to and then turned back to Jess. "She's stable, but they're keeping her sedated for now. It'll be some time before they can determine anything further. You should go home and rest, sweetie."

Jess gave her a silent nod. "Can you please call me and let me know if her condition changes? Her family won't be here for a few days."

Michael winced at her pleading tone. His heart broke for her.

"Of course," the nurse replied.

Michael took Jess's arm and guided her out of the room. "She's in good hands."

The walk to the parking garage was silent. Both took turns sipping their coffees as they made their way to his police cruiser on the upper level.

He unlocked the door and climbed inside. Jess slid into the passenger seat, slamming the door shut. Her hip pressed against it. He didn't blame her for wanting to keep her distance. Holding her in such an intimate way was a big mistake. They weren't a couple anymore. No matter how right it felt.

"Ready?" He asked.

She nodded, keeping her gaze forward. The look of worry seemed to deepen on her face. He could see that she was having a hard time leaving her friend.

"She'll be okay." Michael gave her hand a quick squeeze. It probably wasn't the best move, but she needed to know she wasn't alone in all this.

"It shouldn't have happened in the first place." She shut her eyes tightly.

He wasn't sure if it was to keep herself from crying or because she imagined the state her friend was in. He scrambled to think of something to counteract her reasoning. But it was too easy to relate to how she felt. There were so many things that *shouldn't have happened* but had, and there was nothing he could do to change the past.

"I know what you mean."

Jess turned in his direction, sliding her back partially onto the window, so she was facing him. Michael navigated each block with precision. He knew these streets well.

"You do?" She asked.

He glanced at her, noticing the confusion on her face. Her perfect face. From her ebony hair to her dark exotic eyes to the cupid's bow that shaped her lips. Being with her again brought back so many memories.

"Yeah. I've had a lot of things happen to me in my life that shouldn't have happened. I can dwell on it and wonder why, or I can move forward and see that those things made me stronger and that it was part of God's plan."

"Part of God's plan?" Jess scoffed. "You mean God planned for Tammy to be attacked and for Annabelle to be murdered?"

"No." He gripped the steering wheel.

Please don't let me mess this up. He mentally prayed.

"I'm just saying, we make choices in our lives that result in consequences. Good or bad. We have free will to make those choices. I've found it easier to do that with God's guidance."

"Tammy didn't choose this," Jess shot back.

"No, she didn't. But I'm sure there's a reason it happened." That sounded so cliché, but he couldn't deny the truth of it. Joseph in the Bible was a perfect example. Instead of firing another shot at him as he expected, she turned and stared out the window.

The rest of the trip back to Oakwood Springs was silent. He hoped she was thinking about what he'd said. The last six months of attending church in Oakwood Springs taught him a lot. His choices got him into a bad situation with Tiffany, but God helped him escape it.

He wasn't good enough for Jess, but she was back in his life for a reason. God had forgiven him, but now he could try and earn her forgiveness. He searched for something they could talk about.

"Where did you and Tammy meet?" was what he settled on.

"College." Her murmured response was so low he'd barely heard her.

"I don't remember her." He frowned in thought, going through all the memories he could pull to the surface at a moment's notice.

The woman he'd seen lying in the hospital bed wasn't in any of them.

"I met her after...."

Even though she didn't say it, he knew the rest of that sentence. It cut deep. The glimmer of hope that someday she could forgive him, and he could say that breaking up with her was the biggest mistake of his life was starting to fade.

But this wasn't the same girl he'd left. The girl he left was timid and shy. The girl he left always wore a smile and acted as if she didn't have a care in the world. She was a free spirit. But this girl...this woman sitting next to him, had seen some difficult times, and she'd faced them alone because of him. This Jess seemed a lot stronger. She had to be to have escaped the hands of a cold-blooded killer without a scratch on her.

He recalled one instance where a mouse had made its way into the off-campus apartment she and Tiffany shared. She called him, screaming for him to come and kill it. He had to laugh at the way she was acting over a little mouse. Part of him was glad she called him because it made him feel needed—like he was her hero.

"I live in Chestnut Crest Apartments." Jess's voice sliced into his thoughts.

He glanced over to see her pointing at a sign coming into view with a large white arrow facing left. The name on the sign was also white with loopy cursive and a small illustration of a chestnut perched under it. He'd never been on this side of town.

"Wow, fancy sign." He glanced at her once again, hoping his attempt to break the ice was fruitful.

Nothing.

She didn't so much as look his way. As he made the turn into the parking lot, she pointed to the apartment in the far corner. "Unit A."

Three identical buildings stood surrounding them. At the end, where Jess pointed, was the last structure before the lot opened to a massive field. Michael climbed out of the car with a groan. He was sore from riding so long.

He rounded the hood of the car, reaching out to open the door for her just like he'd done when they were dating. Why did that habit suddenly come back?

She quickly pulled on the door handle and shoved it open. "I don't need your help."

He raised his hands in surrender and stood at the front of the car, waiting to follow her. She fumbled with her keys, chose one, then unlocked the door. She stood at the threshold for a moment, staring into the dark-framed window that led to the stairwell inside, her breathing growing heavier. She was afraid to step into her own home. He wanted to grab her hand and let her know that he was there for her, but he didn't. He doubted she would accept his encouragement. Her words echoed in his mind.

I don't need your help.

"We don't have to go in there right now, Jess. I've got somethings you can use at—"

"I'm on the second floor!" Her voice was shaky, but he knew the more he tried to pull her in one direction, the more she would fight to go the other.

Michael watched her start up the dark stairwell and disappear into the darkness. He stumbled over a step, trying to keep up with her. He didn't want her getting too far from his reach just in case the killer was waiting for them inside. A hand grabbed his upper arm in the darkness. He could make out Jess's small frame near the door.

"You're at the top now," her voice informed him.

"Thanks."

She fumbled with her keys once more. This time, it took a little longer due to the pitch black hallway.

"They told me they'd fixed that light." She grunted, her shaky voice turning annoyed.

"Maybe you'd better let me go inside first. Just in case." Michael stepped past her when she finally got the door opened.

She flipped the light switch next to the door. The sudden brightness of the room revealed just what he'd expected. The living room area was littered with papers and overturned furniture. The curtains had been torn down, and several holes had been kicked into the plaster. Whoever did this must've been angry.

Jess gasped behind him. He pulled his pistol from his belt, quickly searching the apartment. Each room had been torn apart as if whoever did this was looking for something. Papers, books, and boxes were piled in every corner. In the bedroom, old photographs were scattered. Most of them were from their time together in college. He saw a dozen versions of his younger self with an arm around Jess's waist. Some of the photos had Tiffany's face in them too.

Instead of talking to her about the photos, he decided to act like he never saw them. Because he wasn't actually meant to see them. He'd just have to let it eat at him. Why would she keep these photos after the way their relationship ended?

"There's no one here," he announced when he found Jess standing in the kitchen.

Tears dripped onto a bright yellow card she was holding in her hand.

"What's that, Jess?"

"It's my fault," she whispered. He pried the card from her shaking hand.

Jess,

I hope you take me up on next weekend. I have so much to tell you, and I'm dying for you to come and visit.

See you soon!

Love, Tammy.

CHAPTER 6

"That was on my fridge." Jess wrapped her arms around herself as she paced the compact kitchen floor.

It must be how the killer found Tammy. Obviously, that would be the first place she'd go, especially with the polaroid picture next to it of the two of them at the beach with 'Tammy's favorite' written across the bottom.

How could she not remember Tammy's card? It had been held to the fridge by two flower magnets for the last week and a half. But why would he tear her place apart like this? What could he possibly have been looking for?

The image of Tammy's motionless body lying in the hospital came slamming back into Jess's mind. She could die because of her. She'd betrayed her best friend.

Michael rested his hands on her shoulders, pulling her in front of him so he could look her in the eye. "This isn't your fault, Jess. You need to know that. And he's not going to have the chance to hurt anyone else. I promise you. I'm going to keep you safe."

His words made all the sense in the world, but they didn't remove any of the guilt she felt. She was responsible for Annabelle and now Tammy.

"How can you make a promise like that? My whole job is based on helping women in abusive situations and looking at what happened. Hayden's right. I'm a jinx," Jess shot back.

Michael pulled her into a hug. "You are *not* a jinx. Don't listen to comments like that. Besides, there's no such thing."

She squirmed, a little uncomfortable with him being so close. She drew in a deep breath. Her chest heaved from how terrified she was. After a moment, a cool calmness, almost like relaxation, washed over her. She buried her face in his chest, hoping he didn't see the downpour of tears staining her cheeks.

"I think we need to get you back to my place. You could use some rest," Michael muttered softly.

"I'm not safe anywhere. So I might as well just stay here." She was a dead woman walking. Covering her face with her palms, she dropped to her knees on the floor.

"No, you're coming to my house. I told Tom that I'd protect you, and I intend to keep my promise. We're gonna catch this guy, Jess. You need to trust me." Michael held out his hand, pulling her back to her feet.

Trust him? Now she was certain he'd lost his mind. She pulled from his grasp and marched into her bedroom. It took her only a few minutes to put together a bag that would get her through the next few days. She had no idea how long this would last.
About an hour later, she entered Michael's log cabin-like house once again. The smell of leather and cedar greeted her. She had to give it to him—his place was homey and warm. Michael may have been right about this place being the safest spot for her.

"You can have the bedroom. I'll sleep on the couch." Michael clasped his hands together.

Was he nervous about her being here? It wasn't her idea at all, but it didn't seem like he was nervous about his own safety in the situation.

"You want anything to eat or drink?" He pointed both his thumbs toward the kitchen. The way his body curved as he pointed reminded her of those balloon men that whipped back and forth in front of the used car lot.

Jess bit back a smile. "Just some coffee would be fine."

He nodded, then dashed into the kitchen.

Although it still felt awkward that this was Michael she was staying with, maybe she could actually let down her guard a little bit with him. He couldn't do anything worse than what he'd already done to her. Jess let her bag drop to the floor next to the couch, settling herself directly in the center. From this spot, she had a view of the entire living room.

It was well lit with four identical rustic lamps, each positioned on the end tables that were scattered around the room. Forest green curtains covered the windows, making it difficult to see in or out. Knowing no one could see her sleeping made her feel a little bit safer.

A large stone fireplace took up most of the wall to her right. A few logs were positioned off to the side in a brass stand. She was kind of surprised he was still using it this late in spring.

"Nice place you have," she called to the kitchen as she drew in another breath of leather. This was the kind of home Michael had always talked about building for them. He promised her the world. No, she had to keep thoughts of the things he used to say out of her head. She had to make the best of this and remembering wasn't going to help.

"Thanks. It's all finally coming together," he called back from the kitchen. A moment later, he returned with two steaming mugs. He handed one to her that was shaped like a largemouth bass, the lips of the fish forming the rim of the cup.

She laughed. "Thanks for sharing your fine china with me."

"Sorry. That was given to me as a gag gift. I haven't had a chance to wash dishes. I wasn't expecting company." His face flushed, and he adjusted himself on the couch with a small bounce. "There's something I need to talk to you about."

She squared her jaw, holding her breath. He was acting a little nervous, which told her he was going to ask her something she didn't want to answer.

"This morning, you and Tom were sitting right here on the couch. You told him what you saw—what happened, I mean. But you had a look on your face." Michael stared at her for a moment as if he was waiting for her to read his mind.

"What do you mean? What look?"

"Like there was more to the story than what you told us," he said.

"You think I lied about what happened?" Jess stood to her feet, nearly spilling her coffee.

"No. Like there was something you were afraid to say. If there's something else about this case that you know, you need to tell us. It'll only help us bring this guy in quicker." Michael stood too, looking down at her. His eyes searched her face.

He was right. She would have to tell him that Annabelle Mason was the Annabelle she'd thrown to the wolves when they were thirteen. She'd covered this case by mere chance, so it wasn't really relevant, but maybe it would ease her guilt slightly to talk about it. Who knows, It might help them narrow down who could've wanted her dead.

Jess settled herself back onto the couch. "I think Annabelle Mason was someone I knew a long time ago," she began.

Michael's face twitched in confusion. Was he trying to hide the fact that her response surprised him? She told him about how she and Annabelle met and about the disappearance of her mother. Michael listened intently to her story, asking the occasional question. She felt like she was taking down the walls around her heart and showing the world what a bad friend she'd been to Annabelle, a trait that had followed her to adulthood.

"So there could be more to this guy than him simply trying to kill you because you witnessed the murder?" Michael rubbed the stubble on his chin with his free hand.

"I don't know. It seems unlikely to me because I wasn't actually supposed to be there. I was covering for someone." Things were getting more complicated by the minute. She rubbed her temple with her fingertips.

"Still, the connection between you two is worth checking into," he replied, placing his mug on the solid oak coffee table that was pressing against her knees. He stood and marched toward his jacket on the coat rack behind the door. Michael pulled his phone from his pocket and called the station.

He repeated their conversation and named a few things for them to check into. One of them was to look into Annabelle's past to see if she lived in Richmond as a child. The phone call was short and sweet. After he hung up, he sat back on the couch next to her.

"They told me there are only two suspects so far. If we add her father to the list, that'll make three."

"Two suspects?" Jess had no idea there were already suspects.

"Yes, we picked up her husband lurking around the house while you were on your way to Cincinnati."

She recalled seeing the husband parked outside the shelter demanding to see his wife. She remembered a short, small-framed man with a bad attitude.

"Her husband didn't do it. The killer was taller and thicker," she pointed out.

"I know that. I saw the guy too and spoke to him. But to find him poking around right after his wife is murdered does make it seem like he might be involved in some way. Maybe he hired the guy."

She had to admit that Michael's reasoning was sound. She remembered reading in Annabelle's case file that her husband had choked her on more than one occasion. Maybe he did want her dead. The large barrel-chested figure she'd encountered seemed like he had a plan. One she foiled. He'd stabbed Annabelle in a precise location ending her life quickly. When she came into the kitchen, he was standing next to the back door, just out of sight of the front.

"Is there anything else you can tell me about Annabelle that might shed some light on this case?" Michael asked, interrupting her deductions.

"According to her file, Annabelle did have a drug problem, but she was getting help for that." Jess gulped down the last sip of coffee and set the fish mug down on the table.

"Is there anything else you can remember about her? Even seeing her in the grocery store could be important."

She shook her head. "I'm sorry, Michael."

It had been a long and difficult day, and she couldn't think anymore.

"It's alright, Jess. Maybe you should get some rest." He grabbed their coffee cups and took them into the kitchen.

After a few moments and a few bangs, she realized he'd started washing the dishes.

She stood and joined him in the kitchen. "What if he tries something tonight?" Her voice had a quiver of fear in it that there wasn't any point in hiding.

Michael's glance at her was not only full of sympathy but something else— something she couldn't read.

"Would it make you feel better if I stayed up tonight and kept watch?" He stayed focused back on the pot he was scrubbing in his sudsy hands.

Jess bit her lip. "It's alright. I really need to get a grip anyway. Tom wouldn't have sent me here if he didn't trust you to do your job."

She turned and left the kitchen before he could answer. She grabbed her duffel bag off the floor and went into the bedroom Michael pointed out for her to use earlier. She was gonna make it through this. Tammy and Annabelle deserved justice. She had to make it through this.

*****

Michael finished washing all the dishes about twenty minutes after Jess went to bed. After a quick check to make sure the back door was locked, he shut off the kitchen light and went into the living room.

As he went around the room, shutting off all the lamps but one, he thought about everything Jess had told him. If this was the same Annabelle from her childhood, then this case could be more complicated than he'd first thought.

As the sunlight started to brighten the curtains, Michael settled himself on the couch. There wasn't any point in him trying to rest now. He didn't know how long Jess would rest either, so he figured it may be a good idea to try and figure out if Linus Mason was involved or not. He picked up his phone from the coffee table and dialed Harry again. "Hey. What have you figured out?" he asked as soon as someone picked up.

"Well, good morning to you too," Harry quipped.

"Knock it off," he shot back. He was tired and wasn't in the mood for jokes, especially since this was Jess's life on the line.

"I see you didn't get any sleep either," Harry rustled some papers in the background.

Michael pulled the phone away from his ear until the sound stopped.

"Okay. So, apparently Annabelle Mason did live in Richmond as a child with her mom and dad. The mom vanished when Annabelle was about thirteen. The dad was under suspicion for about a year after that. They thought he may have had something to do with her disappearance. Annabelle and her dad moved away from Richmond not long after her mom left. They moved around a lot until she married Linus Mason about six years ago, and they've traveled all over the place together."

Harry's information on Annabelle matched a lot of what Jess had told him.

"They traveled with Annabelle's dad?" Michael asked.

"Um, no. We haven't been able to locate him yet," The horrible sound of rustling papers filled his ears again, causing him to pull the phone away.

"What about Linus?" Michael asked.

If he was involved in any way, they needed to prove it fast, so they had more to hold him on.

"Nothing. He was out of town visiting some friends when his wife was killed. The court order from their domestic violence case wouldn't allow him near the house, and his friends confirmed his alibi," Harry explained.

That was odd. Why would he be poking around his house if, by law, he wasn't supposed to be there? He was going to catch this killer, but he knew Linus was somehow involved, and he was going to find out how.

CHAPTER 7

Darkness surrounded her. Her body ached inside and out, making it extremely difficult to breathe. She tried walking, but it seemed to be impossible as if she was wading in a pool of thick liquid that was up to her chest. The heat made her question if the "pool" was full of lava. Beads of sweat dripped down her face. What's going on? Where was she? Voices called to her from a distance. She wanted to answer, to call for help, but for some reason, her voice came out in raspy groans. She couldn't tell which direction the voices were coming from. She dragged her feet along, pulling them with all her strength.

Run, Jess. He's coming for you. A voice in the distance called to her. She wasn't sure, but it sounded a lot like Tammy.

"Tammy!" She called out into the murky fog covering her eyes.

"*I* will *find her.*" said another voice. This particular voice belonged to a man and rang louder as if it was a whole lot closer. Jess's heart pounded like it was going to burst from her chest. She tried lifting her feet from the bog, but before she could take another step, a hand gripped her shoulder.

"Let go of me!" She screamed, tugging and pulling away.

She wasn't going to let him get away with this. She would *not* be his next victim. The hand let go of her as a light caught her view. Jess forced herself to turn in the mire toward the light, where a silhouette of a young girl appeared.

"Jess, help me!" the girl called to her.

She instantly knew who it was. The very person she'd tried to forget about for most of her adult life. The person who was the reason she became a social worker.

"Annabelle?" Jess called back to the girl. She had to protect her from whoever was chasing her. She'd almost reached her when the girl vanished.

"No! Annabelle!" Jess cried, burying her face in her hands.

"Jess!" another voice echoed through her head. It wasn't Tammy's voice. Nor was it whoever was after her. This one was different. It was bold and clear. She could trust it. "Jess, wake up."

Her eyes came open. The darkness was gone.

"Huh? Michael?" She groaned, rubbing her eyes. He had his hands on both her shoulders. She shoved the center of his chest, pushing him away. His hands released her, then he took a few steps back. That must've been the hand she felt in her dream. Jess let out a sigh of relief. She was safe, for now. "You must've had a nightmare. You screamed." Michael awkwardly scratched the side of his neck.

"Sorry. I guess I did." She looked down at her feet. The blanket had wrapped itself tightly around them. No wonder she couldn't move.

Michael came back over and sat on the side of the bed. She stared at the movement of her tapping toes under the blanket for a few seconds. What a horrible dream.

"Thank you for waking me up, but I'm alright now." She didn't mean for that to come out so grumpy. Jess drew her legs to her chest and wrapped her arms around them. The sunshine pouring in the large window made her feel a little better. She'd half expected to see darkness, like in her dream. It seemed so real.

"Good afternoon, sleepyhead." He said, noticing her staring out the window. His chipper tone told her that he was attempting to cheer her up. Which was something the old Michael did.

She'd felt alone most of her life, which is pretty easy to do if you were an only child. But she couldn't remember the last time she felt *this* alone—like the world was swallowing her up into a black hole. She buried her face in her knees to hide the tears running down her face.

Michael touched her elbow, and warmth radiated through it. She lifted her head, catching his gaze.

"You can talk to me about the dream if you want," he offered.

She shook her head. It was hard enough dealing with him being here when she was in such a vulnerable state. There might've been a time when she'd shared everything with him, even her deepest darkest secrets. But he'd lost that right.

She envisioned herself from Michael's perspective. She must've looked like a morning monster. A pale ghostly form with wiry hair sticking out in all directions. Her cheeks warmed. She pulled her hair out of her face, trying to make herself look more presentable without him noticing.

"Well, I'm here if you need anything." He stood up from the bed.

She was half tempted to make a sarcastic remark in response but quickly reminded herself that he was a police officer just doing his job, and she was a witness to a murder. Her being in his house was strictly business, and it was best if they kept it that way.

"What time is it?" She leaned over to the nightstand in search of her phone—anything to hide from the awkwardness between them.

"About 1:00 p.m.," he said.

Jess nearly let out a shriek. She shot up out of bed. Her boss was going to kill her for not showing up for work this morning. Kill. That word had a whole new meaning for her now. She would have to remember to remove it from her daily vocabulary.

"Get out! I need to get dressed for work." She grabbed her duffel bag and made a dash for the bathroom door.

"What makes you think you're going to work?" He crossed his arms. "You're not going anywhere."

She stopped and turned back to him. He must've thought she was out of her mind. She probably was. Going to work was basically giving the killer an open opportunity to take her out. But she wanted to make sure she had a job to go back to when this was over. If she was alive when this was over that is.

"I can't just not work, Michael. As much as I would like to. I have bills to pay. I figured you'd be coming with me," she called to him through the bathroom door.

He didn't respond. Maybe he was considering it. Jess felt a small spark of hope. Yes, Michael was appointed to protect her, but that didn't mean he could order her around. And she wasn't about to let him start.

After a wonderful hot shower and some clean clothes, Jess felt as if she could take on the world. The steamy hot water seemed to wash away some of her fear and worry as well. If this person wanted to get away with Annabelle's murder, then he wouldn't hang around town this long just to make sure she was silenced too. She hadn't really seen anything to incriminate him anyway. Maybe he'd already left town.

When she exited the bedroom, she caught the scent of seasoned chicken and veggies coming from the kitchen. She drew in a deep breath, then followed her nose. Michael was assembling two plates of grilled chicken salad.

"Not exactly the breakfast I was expecting." She pulled a chair from the table and plopped down in it.

"Actually, this is lunch. You slept through breakfast." Michael set the plate in front of her before disappearing back into the kitchen.

Jess waited awkwardly. She wasn't sure if she should go ahead and eat or wait for him. It was, after all, his house. The refrigerator door swung open and closed, and he came back with two glasses of iced tea, and a bottle of ranch dressing tucked between his fingers.

"Wow, I don't remember you cooking this much," Jess commented.

"I was around you all the time. I didn't have to. You were always whipping up something fantastic," he responded.

Jess dropped her head, instantly regretting her remark. The last thing she wanted to do was talk about how things used to be. She didn't know how long she would have to stay with him, but it was for the best that they avoided the past. She tried to think of something else to say that would lead the conversation away from how inseparable they were, but nothing came to mind. With her head still tilted forward, she stole a peek at Michael, who was fully focused on his meal. He must not have known what to say either.

She couldn't help but think this was just as awkward for him as it was for her. Maybe that was why they ate in silence. When they were together, she used to daydream about getting married and having a house in the country, just like this one. She used to imagine herself cooking for Michael and them sitting down to meals as a family. She never would've guessed them having dinner under these circumstances.

Jess hurried through the rest of the meal. She couldn't stand the uncomfortable silence any longer. She stood, grabbed her plate, and carried it to the sink.

"I can do that," Michael blurted out as she rinsed her plate and fork.

"I've got it." She responded, placing her now clean dishes on the drying rack. Michael finished his last bite and brought his dishes over to the sink as well.

"Hand them over," She reached out to take them. He pulled them out of her reach playfully. "I usually don't make guests do the dishes."

"I'm not exactly a guest. I figure it's best if I at least earn my keep." She tried to ignore the tingle in her arm as she reached over his shoulder to take the plate. Her face was close to his. Dangerously close.

Jess took a few steps back as her face grew warm. Her cheeks had to be flaming red. Staying with Michael was not going according to plan at all.

"You know what, you go ahead and wash those. I'm gonna go call my boss and let him know what's going on." She turned and hurried out of the kitchen before he could say anything else.

Jess grabbed her phone off the nightstand in the bedroom.

Hayden Cunningham wasn't a difficult boss to work with, but he wasn't an easy one either. There were good days and bad. How was she supposed to tell him that she would have to take a few weeks' vacation on such short notice? Even if he'd already heard what happened to Annabelle Mason. But she had no choice, not if she liked being alive.

She dialed Hayden. While it rang, she prayed he wouldn't still be upset with her for spending the entire day up at Safe Haven last week. One of the girls had drugs hidden in her room. Jess was simply trying to figure out how she got it. The women living at Safe Haven could come and go as they pleased, to a degree, but no illegal substance of any kind was allowed on the premises.

"Hello?" Hayden's voice cut into her thoughts. He seemed to be in an alright mood until she told him what was going on.

"Are you alright? Where are you?" he asked quickly.

"I can't say, but I thought you should know that you won't see me for a while," she explained.

"Is there anything I can do? Can I bring you anything?"

"No, thanks. I'd just like a job to come back to when this is over," Jess laughed nervously.

She literally just said she couldn't tell him where she was. Typical of Hayden. She could envision him reading a newspaper or scrolling on his computer while talking on the phone. No one ever had his full attention when he was in his office.

"Don't worry about that," He replied. Although his words took a load off her mind, he was almost too understanding about the situation. Something seemed a little off about how he spoke. She couldn't quite put her finger on it, but he wasn't himself.

It may not have been such a good idea to tell him she'd witnessed Annabelle's murder and was under police protection.

"I'm going to grab the stuff Annabelle Mason left up at Safe Haven. The police want it, and sending a cop over there might freak everyone out," she explained.

"No, I'll go today and pick it up. I don't want you leading a killer to Safe Haven," Hayden shot back at her.

Jess's mouth dropped open at the sudden change in his tone. It wasn't as if she was a bad luck charm bringing death to anyone she visited, but his remark made her feel like one.

"It's really no trouble, Hayden. I'm sure you have a lot of things you need to do now that I can't be there," She argued.

"I said I would get it. I don't want you anywhere near Safe Haven, and that's final." The phone beeped, indicating that Hayden had hung up.

She let her hand fall from her ear to her side. Hayden seemed angry at the fact that she wanted to go to Safe Haven and retrieve the last of Annabelle's belongings. Did he really think of her as some kind of jinx? She had enough on her mind right now, hiding from a killer with the one person she was determined to never see or speak to again.

"What did your boss say?" Michael leaned into the doorway.

She searched for the right words. Should she tell him that Hayden didn't want her or the police at Safe Haven and that he was acting suspiciously? That would've been the smart move, but strange things have been going on in Safe Haven for a while. About half of the women staying there hadn't passed the last few drug tests.

Jess was sure that someone working inside of Safe Haven was dealing drugs, but she hadn't been able to find out who. Maybe that was who killed Annabelle. It was a good place to start, at least. "Hayden was acting a little strange. He told me to stay away from Safe Haven," she finally explained.

"Did he say why?"

"He said he doesn't want me leading a killer there." She frowned and tilted her head to the side, deep in thought.

"What are you thinking?" Michael asked.

"I was just telling him that I was going to Safe Haven to get the last of Annabelle's things. She left some stuff there and told Mia she'd be back for it," Jess explained.

"Why didn't she just take it with her?"

That was a question Jess had asked herself several times since Mia told her about Annabelle's odd request. She wasn't sure if it had anything to do with the drugs found in some of the girl's belongings.

"I don't know," she said, unable to give Michael a reasonable answer from the questions and details swirling around in her head.

"Maybe she wanted something to be kept safe from someone," Michael suggested.

"But who?"

"That's a good question. One worth looking into." He started toward the door, then stopped and looked over his shoulder. "You coming?"

Jess stood and followed him. "Wait, Hayden said he'd retrieve her things. If he sees me there...."

"He won't say anything if you're with me," Michael said.

She didn't know how to respond. Michael's tone was more like, *He'd better not say anything if you're with me.*

"Okay." She followed him out the front door.

She wasn't sure why, but she didn't fully trust Hayden. He didn't pay much attention to the job, nor did he seem to care much about what happened to the women after they left Safe Haven. The only reason he got the job was because his mother was the mayor and hoped it would keep him out of trouble.

A twinge hit her stomach as she climbed into Michael's truck. What if he was right about not leaving his house? Maybe she shouldn't go to Safe Haven. The killer could follow them there and put more lives in danger.

Yes, going to Safe Haven could reveal something about Annabelle's life that might indicate who would want her dead, but it could also lead her right into the killer's hands. She wasn't sure if putting herself at that kind of risk was worth it, but she didn't have much choice at this point.

It would take them about twenty minutes to get back to town. Michael turned out of his driveway and onto the small two-lane road. Jess couldn't help but watch Annabelle's house as they passed by. Her heart grew heavy. She kept telling herself that there wasn't anything she could have done to save Annabelle. Still, she felt like she'd abandoned her there on the kitchen floor.

She glanced over at Michael. He wore a sober expression. Was he thinking about the brutal murder of his neighbor? Did he blame himself for not seeing that he was talking to a murderer? Jess took in a deep, shaky breath. She was putting her job and her life in his hands. Could he handle such a responsibility?

*****

Michael followed every direction Jess gave. He had to admire her for working for such a needed cause. He'd seen too many women beaten and even killed by their husbands. He could relate to it as well. About three years ago, Tiffany filed a complaint against him for domestic violence when she was the one who'd hit him. No one bothered to ask why his eye was blackened.

The complaint nearly cost him his job. Thank heaven his boss believed his story instead of the police report that stated he'd run into something. That wasn't the first time Tiffany caused problems for him there. Which was why he ended up leaving Cincinnati.

"This is it," Jess said in almost a whisper.

He pushed his own problems aside and focused on parking the truck. She shoved her hands under her thighs. He suspected it was to hide their shaking.

Once the truck was parked, his upper body twisted toward her. "You don't have to do this. I can get a court order and have all Annabelle's things sent over to the sheriff's office."

She pressed her lips together as if thinking about his suggestion. He wanted to grab her hand and tell her that he would be there for her no matter what. But he didn't. He couldn't bear her pulling it away.

Jess shook her head. "No, I have to do this. I can't just keep hiding. Besides, I need to check on my girls." She opened the passenger side door and stepped out.

Michael followed at her heels, making sure he could push her out of the way if something happened.

The smell of broiled chicken greeted them when they entered the group home. He had no idea what to expect. It wasn't the nicest house on the block, but if everyone in Oakwood Springs knew what it stood for—women who'd taken their lives back and made a fresh start—then they would see its beauty. If only he'd had some support system like this when he was with Tiffany.

"Jessie! Oh, I'm so glad to see you. I heard you would be taking some time off. What are you doing here?" A woman who looked to be about ten years older than him was standing in the living room. She was heading for a long hallway where some voices were coming from.

"Hi, Marge. I'm helping the police answer a few questions about Annabelle Mason. Do you still have her things here?" Jess's chipper self returned as if rehearsed.

"Oh yes, I knew her moving back home would only be a temporary thing. So I left her things in her room. I was going to pack them up today when I heard she'd...." She sniffled. "The poor dear. She was such a sweet girl."

Marge rambled on as he took the opportunity to have a look around. The open living room, lined with several chairs, looked more like something that would seat a large family instead of abused women seeking shelter.

Taking a peek down the hallway, he spotted several women standing around in the kitchen talking in hushed voices. He smiled and nodded at them.

"You can go on up and get whatever you need," Marge said.

Jess turned to him with a smile. "I'll be right back."

Before he could protest, Marge approached him. "Are the rumors true? Was Annie murdered?" she whispered.

"Where did you hear that from?" Michael asked with a small cough. He wasn't a very good liar, but he wasn't supposed to talk about an open investigation.

"It's not hard to put two and two together. She started acting funny when we hired a maintenance worker to come and spray the house. Termites can get nasty if they aren't dealt with. Then the same man came by a few days later to talk to Annabelle. It caused quite a stir here. She wasn't the same after that. Next thing we know, she's dead, and you all are looking into her death. I believe he had something to do with it."

Michael nodded along as she spoke but was doing his best to listen for Jess to come back down the stairs.

His nerves twisted tighter as he counted the seconds since she'd left the room.

"Did Annabelle leave a lot here?" He interrupted.

"No, just a few small things." She blinked. "Why?"

"Excuse me for a second. Which room did Ms. Mason stay in?" He started for the stairs.

"First room to the right. Go on up. All the girls are in the kitchen having lunch," she instructed.

As he reached the top of the stairs, he called for Jess, praying she would answer him. He waited. No answer.

"Jess," he called again as he entered the room.

Jess came to the door, huffing and gasping for breath.

"He's here!" She wheezed.

Michael pushed past her, nearly sending her into the wall. He should've known better than to let her come up here alone. What was he thinking?

He caught sight of a man in a green jumpsuit running down the street. He must've climbed into the window in order to get into the house unnoticed. Michael nearly dove down the stairs to get outside in time to see which way he went.

Once outside, he ran as fast as he could. How did he know that Annabelle would be staying here? That information was usually on a need-to-know basis. When he reached the street, the green jumpsuited figure ran down, his head darted in each direction. There was no way to tell which way he'd gone from here, but from what he could see of his body type, it was the same man that was in the woods yesterday morning.

Michael stopped running at the four-way stop, looking for some indication as to which way the killer ran. It wasn't looking like he'd bring him in today. He'd better get back to Safe Haven and take Jess down to the station to give a formal statement. While they were there, they could go over a new plan to keep her safe. He would also have to explain to Tom that he really dropped the ball on this one. That wasn't something he was looking forward to.

CHAPTER 8

Michael returned to the group home, wearing a look of defeat. The killer had gotten away. The warmth of Marge's hand rubbing her back was the only thing keeping her from losing it. It was comforting. She seemed like that kind of lady. One that would feel like a second mother to anybody. It had to be why she was so good at her job.

"I've called the Sheriff," Marge said.

"Thanks. Can you let the girls in the kitchen know that everything is alright and not to worry? I don't want anyone freaking out because of all the cops coming and going in here." Michael asked, pointing toward the kitchen.

"Of course."

Once Marge was out of sight, Michael seated himself on the couch next to Jess. "You okay?"

"*Okay?* No, I'm not *okay*! I thought he was going to kill me before you even knew he was here." How on earth could he ask her that?

"Look, I'm really sorry, but we're gonna have to do more in order to keep you safe. That was too close a call."

She could almost detect pain behind his eyes, along with the same fear and protectiveness she used to see when they were dating. Or was she just wanting to see those things?

"He grabbed me by my throat. He was hiding behind the door, Michael. He was here the whole time."

"Did you see his face?" Michael's eyes widened.

"No, he was wearing a medical mask-like before," She burst out, throwing herself into his arms. She couldn't hold back the sobs any longer.

His arms squeezed her. For a moment, she thought her life was over.

He pulled her from his chest, looking her in the eye. "I promise you that we're gonna catch this guy. I'm going to catch him. And I'm not gonna let you out of my sight again until this is over."

His tone brought back the memory of promises he'd made to her before. Promises he'd broken. She'd trusted him then, and it cost her a large part of her heart. She didn't want to trust him now, but if she didn't, it could cost her life.

Michael squeezed her shoulders, then pulled her into a soft kiss. He brushed his full lips against hers then leaned back to look at her again.

She stared at him, unsure of what just happened was real or not. No, she wasn't going to let him get in her head. She pulled away from his grasp. They shouldn't be doing this. She tried to tell him this, but her lips wouldn't form words. They were still warm from his kiss.

Michael turned and stood. A twinge of regret hit her stomach. Why would he do that? This was the worst possible time to be romantic. Or maybe it was just the right time. She didn't feel as frightened as she did a few moments ago. She felt safe. Maybe that was his intention. She remembered a homework assignment they worked on in that first psychology class they took together, redirecting someone's attention as a coping mechanism.

"C'mon. I'm gonna take you down to the station." He kept his back to her as he led her to the door.

If only he would turn so she could see what he was really feeling. Was she really another job to him? Surely, he wasn't so calloused. Why did it bother her that he acted so indifferent after kissing her? She was supposed to hate him.

"Jessie, are you alright?" Tom's voice came from the doorway.

Jess ran into his arms. "Yes. Michael scared him off before he could do any real damage."

He turned to Michael, his jaw clenched. "You need a few more lessons in protecting witnesses, Redman."

"It wasn't his fault. I did something stupid. I should've known something like this would happen. This guy's out to get me, and I—" She couldn't let him take the blame when she insisted on coming here in the first place.

"Either way, you're riding back to the station with me." Tom led her to an open car door. He didn't utter a word for the entire trip. She kept glancing behind them at Michael's truck. He couldn't get in trouble because of bad judgment on her part. They'd gotten a little too comfortable. *She'd* gotten a little too comfortable.

Once they arrived at the police station, a young officer named Harry took her statement. She spoke slowly to make sure she remembered every detail.

"I entered the room Annabelle stayed in and was about to go to the closet on the far wall. He was hiding behind the door. He grabbed my throat and squeezed," her hand went to her throat as she explained the rest of the scene.

"He would've killed me if Michael hadn't come in," she finished. Harry's fingers tapped the keyboard in front of him, glancing at her from time to time to indicate he was still listening. His manner seemed kind but distracted. He was still typing away when she finished. She glanced over his shoulder to see Tom talking to Michael in his office. She really didn't want him to get fired. She needed to talk to both of them and tell them about her phone call to Hayden. It was probably nothing, but he was the only person who knew she was going to Safe Haven for Annabelle's things.

"Is that all you need?" Jess asked the eager young deputy.

"Yeah, I believe so. Unless there's anything else, you can remember that might be helpful to the case."

"No. That's all. I'm gonna pop in and talk to Tom for a minute if that's okay." Jess stood and crossed the room, opening the door to Tom's office before the young deputy could stop her.

From the expressions both men were wearing, she must've interrupted something very important.

"What's going on?" She asked, standing in the open doorway.

Two sets of big, concerned eyes stared at her.

"C'mon, guys. I'm right in the middle of all of this. I wanna be kept in the loop."

The pleading in her voice caused both of them to soften. She hated feeling so vulnerable.

"You might as well sit down, Jessie. Michael was just getting me up to speed about one of our suspects." Tom gestured toward the chair.

"Linus Mason didn't do it, but I'm certain he's involved," Michael said. He made a fist as he spoke.

"I have to release him then. We don't charge people based on a hunch."

"I understand that, but—"

"What you really should be focused on is who tried to kill Jessie today. It's likely the same person who killed Annabelle Mason," Tom twitched his mustache back and forth while rubbing his chin. It was what he did when he wasn't sure about his next move. It didn't happen often, but it was happening now on a case involving her. They couldn't afford to be uncertain about anything when it came to a vicious murderer.

"I *am* focused on that. I'm just saying I think Linus Mason hired the guy who killed Annabelle," Michael said.

"Great theory. But can you prove it? The D.A. is only interested in facts," A twinge of frustration rose in Tom's voice.

"Just give me a little more time. If we could hold him for a few more days... I really feel like he's connected to this," Michael pressed.

"Again. We don't have anything to hold him on. In the meantime, I think Jessie needs to go somewhere else—somewhere that's gonna be a lot safer than your house."

Michael's fists were balled up so tightly, that they were starting to turn white. "Um, I thought we discussed—"

Tom cut him off.

"Yes, we did, and I'm giving you an order."

Jess didn't know what to feel. Tom wanted to keep her safe, but was Michael trying to get away from her? She should be glad that he wasn't trying to push anything after the surprise kiss a few hours ago, but it would hurt a little bit if he was.

Tiffany told her all those years ago that she was holding Michael back from his true potential. Not that Tiffany was a good judge of how much potential a person had. She now knew that it was just Tiffany's attempt to justify her actions—stabbing what was supposed to be her best friend in the back.

"I have a cabin about twenty miles south of town. It's secluded, and not too many people know it's there. I go up there every now and then to do a little thinking and fishing. Nobody should be able to find her there." Tom reached into the drawer of his desk and pulled out a small set of keys.

Michael took them and shoved them into his pocket. She could almost see the wheels turning in his head. They had made some sort of plan and were keeping it to themselves. Based on how well she knew them, it was probably because she wasn't going to like it. She would have to let it slide this time, because she had some things planned that neither of them would like either.

*****

Michael didn't really like the scolding he received from Tom but understood why he got it. He and Jess were very close. Closer than he'd realized. As he left the police station, he could feel her following behind.

"I'm not a baby, you know. I can handle myself pretty well. I've done just fine all these years," she muttered.

Michael sighed. This was not the time or place for an argument. "I'm sure you can, Jess. Tom is only trying to protect you. So am I. I don't want anything to happen to you."

He drove his pickup truck out of the parking lot and started heading South toward the cabin.

"Remember when we used to have those movie nights?" Jess was staring out the window. She must've had one memory in particular to bring up their past relationship.

Michael wasn't sure where she was going with the question, so he decided he would tread softly. "Yeah…"

"Well, I hope there's something good on TV because it looks like that's what we're going to be doing for the time being."

"Starting tomorrow night." From the corner of his eye, he saw her turn and face him. His heart fluttered in his chest.

She wasn't going to like what he was about to tell her. He'd broken so many promises he'd made to her. He wasn't about to break another one.

"What do you mean?"

"Harry told me he was able to get an address for the maintenance worker. I'm going to go check it out. It's the best lead we have right now." He admitted, knowing Tom was going to lose it and probably fire him. But he had to make sure he wasn't leaving any stone unturned.

"You're going to do this by yourself?" The twinge of fear in her voice made him question his decision to tell her.

"What, you don't think I can handle it?" He tried to sound as if he was offended at her assumption, but he couldn't really blame her for thinking it.

"I never said that." Jess squirmed in her seat. "What am I supposed to do while you're checking it out?"

His lips pressed together. He promised he wouldn't let her out of his sight, but if he took her with him and she ended up hurt, then he'd never forgive himself. There was no one he trusted enough to stay with her, and Tom would lose it if he found out that he didn't follow orders. No one could protect her like he could. It was a huge risk having her at what could be the killer's house, but he had no choice. The huge risk would have to be taken to keep her safe.

"I guess you'll have to come with me, but promise you'll listen to everything I say."

Making her promise was the only thing he could think of to give him a little peace of mind. He wished there was somewhere else he could send her where he knew she'd be safe. But there wasn't.

CHAPTER 9

A rush of excitement and fear ran through her as Michael navigated his way back to town. He hadn't said much since he told her his plan. Tom would kill him if he knew. But she wasn't going to be the one to tell him. She was grateful to get to tag along. She was tired of running and ached to have her freedom back—the freedom to return to work without worrying someone would choke the life out of her.

Michael's stern expression conveyed that he was deep in thought. She wanted to let him formulate a plan, but the silence made her anxious.

So is the address the only info your friend Harry got on the guy?" She pressed her lips together, studying his profile as she waited for a response.

It looked a lot more rugged than it used to. His lip moved when he was deep in thought. She used to find it adorable. It still kind of was. Watching his lips reminded her of the kiss he'd sprung on her earlier today. She had to admit that she felt something when he kissed her. Something she hadn't felt in a long time. She breathed in, catching the smell of the musk cologne she'd seen him use this morning.

"What?" Michael's voice cut into her thoughts. He'd caught her staring at him.

"I asked you if the address was the only info your friend Harry got on this guy." *Nice save.* She wanted to give herself a good smack for drooling over how handsome he'd gotten in the last five years.

"No, we got a name too. Robert Crawford. But we can't be sure that's his real name." Michael explained.

"He could've used a fake address too," Jess pointed out.

"I've considered that, but I need to check it out to make sure." Michael picked up the notepad he'd scribbled the address on and glanced down at it, then quickly back up at the road.

"You're going to get us killed doing that." She playfully swiped the notepad from his grasp and read the address.

A cold chill crawled through her body. This address wasn't far from where she lived. She could've passed this person a hundred times. This man could be someone she'd spoken to. She thought back to when she was hiding in the bush and tried to remember the killer's voice, even though that was the last thing in the world she wanted to do.

Jess closed her eyes, picturing the view she had of Michael's work boots and the boots the killer wore. Was it boots or sneakers? She couldn't really remember. The important thing right now was remembering his voice. It was deep and a little gravelly, almost like a lion's roar. Each word he spoke struck an icy fear in her heart.

Had she heard it before? Yes, she remembered hearing a voice like that once. But who did it belong to? If they knew her, maybe they had more reason to kill her than witnessing them stab someone. All these questions and more swirled in her head. She was going to get answers.

"What's wrong?" Michael asked.

Jess opened her eyes, holding up the notepad. "Nothing. I know where this is."

Once they were back within the city limits, it only took a few minutes for Michael to navigate to the house. She looked around.

This was the neighborhood where a lot of the girls she cared for came from. He parked his truck about a block down the street. They still had a good view of the house but were far enough away to avoid being noticed.

"This doesn't look like the home of a killer," Jess observed.

The house had a fresh coat of paint. It was white with red shutters and a stone chimney. The yard looked well-kept, and rose bushes lined the front walk.

"Murderers come in all kinds. Gotta keep up appearances to avoid suspicion," Michael said.

"But this place seems *too* nice. I don't like the look of it." Jess crossed her arms. This was the first time a white picket fence gave her the creeps.

"We'll hang out here for a bit and see if our suspect comes home. If he does, I'll call for backup, and we'll nab him."

"And if he doesn't?"

"Then we'll head for the cabin like we're supposed to."

"That's your plan?" She didn't even try to hide her sarcasm.

"Would you rather us get him sooner or later?" He turned his upper body in her direction.

"Sooner, but this is a horrible idea. We should go to the cabin...now." She fired back.

Why was he acting like he had something to prove? Maybe they would catch him here, maybe not. Either way, being here put her life on the line. Was being a hero all that mattered to him? He reached into the back seat, pulling a pair of binoculars from his bag.

"Now, we wait." He held the binoculars up to his eyes and peered through them.

Jess squirmed in her seat. Michael's truck wasn't as comfortable as Tom's police cruiser. Her back and legs ached from sitting for so long. As the minutes turned into hours, the pain grew worse. She rubbed the muscles in her thighs and around her knees, desperately wanting to get out and stretch her legs. The afternoon turned into evening. Michael pulled the binoculars from his face a few times to rub his eyes.

"Have you seen anything?" She finally asked him.

"I thought I did a second ago, but it turned out to be a cat trying to climb into the windowsill." Disappointment colored his voice.

Just as she was about to thank him for risking his job for her, her stomach began to rumble. "Why don't I grab us a bite to eat really quick? It's getting close to dinner time."

"You're crazy if you think I'm letting you get out of this truck" Michael shot her a look.

"I'm just going to grab us a couple of sandwiches in here." She pointed over her shoulder.

They were parked less than five feet from the door to Samuel's deli, which was one of the best sandwich shops in town, in her opinion.

"I'll be in and out in five minutes. Scout's honor." She held up her hand.

Michael's lips pursed as though he was trying to keep his temper. "If this guy is hiding around here somewhere, he could see you and take you out before you even made it to that door. I'm not putting you at risk like that for a sandwich."

She wanted to protest. She would admit that she was terrified for her life, but she wasn't about to live the rest of it looking over her shoulder.

". You stay and watch the house. I'll get the food." Michael shoved the bulky binoculars into her hand and exited before she could respond.

She held them to her eyes, twisting the little knobs until the house came into focus. She pointed them at the upstairs window over the garage. That might be an apartment. Maybe the killer rented it out while they were in town for their unlawful deeds. She froze. Was that movement in the upstairs window? No. Just the cat again. She sighed. Catching this guy was going to be harder than she thought.

If only she had Michael's confidence that the killer would be caught. He seemed confident about *everything* he did. He'd always been that way. That was one of the things she loved most about him. She glanced into the deli and caught sight of his uniformed figure standing directly in front of the counter.

A warm feeling washed over her. Even though things happened the way they did between them, deep down, she still loved him. She sighed again. That was a thought she was going to force herself to bury deep within her heart. So that it would never resurface. Like it was trying to do now.

*****

Michael released the door behind him as he entered. The movement caused the little bell hanging from it to jingle. The shop wasn't very big. Several small ceiling fans hung low, spinning at different speeds. A few tables and chairs lined one side of the room, while a large glass display window filled with meats and cheeses of every possible kind filled the other side. A tall, thin man stood behind the counter wearing a white apron.

"Can I help you?" he asked.

Michael made a quick mental note of his name tag. So this was Sam. He slowly approached the counter, taking one more quick scan of the room. Two figures sat at the very back table, too far away for Michael to hear what they were saying. One of them was wearing a navy blue jacket, and the other was wearing a dark shirt. Was it green? Was this their man? And if it was, who was he talking to and why?

"Need any help deciding?" Sam asked.

Michael was pulled back into reality. "Huh? Oh, I'll have two ham and Swiss sandwiches. To go please."

He shoved his hands into his pockets, wishing he could hear what the two men were saying. Even the smallest detail could indicate if one of them knew anything. He wanted to sneak another peek at them but didn't want to scare them off.

As Sam flipped four pieces of bread down on the wooden countertop, Michael glanced out the front door of the shop. Jess had moved to the driver's side and had the binoculars pointed at the house. He watched her for a moment. She shifted her view here and there, like she was trying to keep an eye on a moving target.

He couldn't imagine any of the women he'd known in his life to be as brave and daring as she was. He should have regretted his decision to bring her on this stakeout with him, but he didn't. Being with her seemed to make everything better. Even the sun shined a little brighter than usual today.

He took another quick glance at the two figures sitting in the back. One of them was now walking toward the front of the shop. He was younger than the man he spoke to in the woods yesterday. The dark shirt turned out to be navy blue.

Not our guy. Michael took a step back so the man could pay for his lunch.

"A great meal, Sam," the man said with a surprisingly deep and gravelly voice.

"Glad you liked it," The two chatted for a moment while Sam finished his order, then he bid Sam good night. Michael watched him as he walked outside and past the truck.

"Here are your sandwiches." Sam placed two large Styrofoam boxes on top of the display case.

Michael took them, paid for their food, then rejoined Jess. He opened the driver's side door and slid in, handing her one of the white boxes. "I got you ham and Swiss."

"I can't believe you remembered." She gave him a shy smile.

"Well yeah. We always got the same thing from the cafeteria at Mountainview."

His explanation caused her smile to slowly fade. He wanted to tell her that he remembered everything about her. The way she laughed. Her favorite movies. How much he missed her. But he couldn't. She'd never forgive him for leaving her the way he did. He'd completely abandoned her when she needed him most and married her best friend. A mistake he was still trying to bounce back from five years later. Jess handed the binoculars to him. He took a bite from his sandwich while watching the house. The cool, smoky flavor made him realize he was hungrier than he'd first thought.

About three hours after he devoured the delicious sandwich, Michael was starting to think this hadn't been such a good idea. They hadn't seen anything in hours. Not even the cat.

"Maybe we should head to the cabin. It's getting dark," Jess pointed out.

She was right. Tom might check up on them, and it would be in the best interest of his job if he didn't find out that Michael had disobeyed his orders.

"Sounds fine with me." He turned the key, causing the car to jump and rumble.

Anger and anxiety whirled like a tornado inside him. They didn't see anything. He would need to come up with a plan for what they should do next. If Linus wasn't involved with his wife's death and they weren't able to catch up with their current suspect, he would need to think of another way of getting information about the maintenance worker. He pulled his phone from his pocket.

"What are you thinking?" Jess asked.

"I just want to check and see if Harry has any new leads on the case." He tapped Harry's name in his contact list and held the phone to his ear.

It rang twice before Harry answered.

"Hey stranger. How do you like your vacation?" Harry quipped.

"Very funny. Have you learned anything new about the case that might help us out?"

Michael asked, half expecting him to say no. He heard some movement.

"I'm not supposed to say anything, but Tom is having us looking into a local drug operation that we just discovered to see if Annabelle Mason's name comes up," Harry explained in a hushed tone.

"And why aren't you supposed to say anything about that?"

"Tom's just worried that you'll want to lead the investigation yourself to impress Ms. Jess."

Michael didn't respond. He didn't want Tom finding out that he'd taken Jess with him on a stakeout that he wasn't supposed to be on.

"I don't think this is going to lead us anywhere, though," Harry continued.

"Why not? It's actually a good idea to figure out where Annabelle got her drugs from. She might have owed someone money, and they came to collect, but she wasn't able to pay." Michael rubbed his stubbled chin.

"I hadn't considered that possibility." Harry's voice brightened at the assumption.

"Just don't tell Tom that it came from me, Harold."

Harry had a heart of gold, but his timid behavior and hyperactive mind tended to get the better of him sometimes. He'd been at the Oakwood Springs Police department for about three months longer than Michael had. But because of Michael's degree, he was able to land the job as Harry's superior. Michael teased him every now and then by calling him Harold but always treated him with respect.

"Let me know what you find out," Michael said before hanging up the phone. He was glad Tom was thinking the same way he was about the case.

Going through the suspect list one at a time wasn't getting him very far. Maybe it would be best to get his mind off this for a little while and see what Harry came up with tomorrow.

As Michael turned the car onto the backroad that led to the cabin, he flipped on his headlights. There weren't streetlights out here, making it difficult to spot any landmarks that might tell him he was going the right way. Just as he was about to ask Jess how her friend Tammy was doing, a flash of light from the rearview mirror hit his eyes. He looked to see a car with dull headlights following them. That was strange. He couldn't recall any houses or farms out here. No one would have any reason to be going this way.

Unless. He glanced back at the road to make sure he was staying on the correct side. He was just about to take another look in the mirror to see the make of the vehicle, but before he could, it sped up. The headlights got closer, ramming into his tailgate.

"What was that?" Jess screeched, turning around to look behind them.

"We're being followed!" Michael slammed his foot on the gas pedal. The engine revved as the truck lurched forward.

The truck behind them matched their speed. He turned the wheel to the left, sending them tilting in that direction. Jess's arms flew out to steady herself. She grabbed the seatbelt strap that was over her shoulder and gave it a firm tug.

Michael looked back in his mirror. He could no longer see the headlights. He whipped his head around just in time to see the truck speeding up to get alongside them. The closer it got, the more he could make out about it. It was a green Ford pickup with a few rust spots just around the right front fender.

Suddenly, the driver swerved, ramming into the side of his truck. Michael turned the wheel, fighting to make sure they didn't hit a tree or end up in a ditch. The mysterious truck rammed into them a second time, then a third. His foot crushed the gas pedal to the point of making his thigh tense. Maybe he could outrun them. This was one time he wished they were in his cruiser. He loved his truck, but it wasn't built for speed.

This was not working. The pursuers were matching their speed. He had to figure out something fast. Calling for backup wasn't going to do them any good and he wasn't about to lead them to the cabin.

He whipped onto the first turn off. The tiny dirt road was full of ruts, sending them hopping and bouncing along. Michael glanced at her hand that was pressed against the ceiling, her failing attempt to stay in the seat. Her knuckles had turned white. The look of sheer terror on her face sent rage through him.

No matter what happened to him, he would keep his promise to her. They would catch this guy.

CHAPTER 10

Jess had lost all feeling in her hands and feet. Her thighs and forearms were burning. She didn't know how much longer she could hold herself in place before succumbing to being tossed around like a rag doll. She prayed the dirt road they were speeding down would turn back into blacktop soon. Could they outrun whoever was chasing them? She turned to get a look at the vehicle but could only see two dim headlights not far behind them.

Michael turned onto a blacktop road. Just like that, her prayers were answered. The engine growled, telling her he was pushing the accelerator to the floor. She wasn't sure where they were or where they were going. It didn't matter, as long as they got away from whoever this was.

Jess took one more look behind them. To her horror, the blacktop had also given their vehicle an advantage.

"They're getting closer!" Tears drifted down her face.

The dark green car sped up then rammed into their rear bumper again. The force of the impact sent her forward into the dashboard. She pushed herself back up into the seat.

"I've got an idea." Michael slammed on the brakes, swerving as the truck slowed.

Has he lost his mind? She glared at him but followed his gaze out her window. The forest they were in before the chase started had turned into fields of tall corn stalks as far as she could see. Michael turned into the field with another massive bump. They came to a screeching halt.

"Follow me. Quick!" Michael pulled his seatbelt off his shoulder.

Jess copied him, then climbed out as quickly as she could. By the time her feet were on solid ground, Michael had circled the front of the truck and grabbed hold of her wrist, pulling her into the cornfield.

The moon shone brightly, lighting up everything except the ground between the corn stalks. Michael pulled her farther into the darkness. She followed almost blindly. As his truck disappeared from sight, headlights lit up the field. Michael stopped in his tracks, then pulled her in another direction to avoid the lights.

When they were a safe distance away, they crouched down. She caught a glimpse of a pistol in his hand. She tried to take deep breaths, so her breathing was quiet.

The tall green stalks rustled about twenty five yards away. They were in the field now... looking for them. The tears running down her face multiplied, making wet spots on the back of her hands which were cupping her knees. She held her breath to stop herself from sobbing. Michael still had his hand wrapped around her wrist. His grip was tight, and she could tell he was slightly trembling. Was he as afraid as she was?

She gripped his shirt as their footsteps got closer. The terror had her insides twisted so tightly, that she'd nearly lost control of her lungs and throat. She gasped, almost letting out a scream. Michael threw a hand over her mouth. The footsteps sounded as if they would walk right up to them, but instead they walked right past.

"I don't think we're gonna find them out here," a familiar voice called in the darkness. It was the killer's voice—a voice that had been haunting her dreams for the last few days. A voice that had her best friend Tammy clinging for her life.

"I know you're hiding out there. I will find you, and I will get you," the voice yelled angrily.

She couldn't stop herself from trembling. Michael wrapped his arms around her, squeezing her tightly. Was he trying to help her stop, or keep her fight or flight instincts from kicking in? Flight in this case. A small part of her hoped that it might be because he wanted to reassure her that she wasn't alone in this and that he would protect her.

"Let's go. This place is gonna be crawling with cops soon. No doubt this one's already called for backup," another voice said. This voice was a lot harder to hear. Yet something seemed familiar about it too.

Jess tried to think of all the women she's helped leave all kinds of abusive situations. A lot of the time, the husband or boyfriend would blame her for the woman leaving. That was something she could never fully understand. These women reached out to her for help. Not the other way around. They finally had enough of being abused and decided to take their lives back. She was simply helping them do that. Was she about to pay the ultimate price for trying to do the right thing?

*****

Michael listened closely to the voices of the two men. He wanted to make sure he remembered them so he would have no problem identifying them later. Things went silent. With each passing second, Alarm grew in the pit of his stomach. He was certain that they were trying to sneak up on them.

This wouldn't be such a bad situation if he were out here on his own. He might've actually met the killers head on and tried to incapacitate them for an arrest. But he wasn't out here alone. The slender figure in his arms hadn't stopped trembling for several minutes. It was a little chilly out here, but he knew it was mostly because she was terrified.

Wishing he knew how to make her feel safe, he slowly rubbed her arm in a comforting gesture. Her breathing started to slow. Eventually, the headlights that had lit up most of the field turned and disappeared.

The killers were gone. Or at least he hoped they were.

Jess buried her face in his chest, letting out the sobs that made her body shake harder.

"It's alright. I wouldn't have let anything happen to you. But we should still keep our voices down," he whispered.

"You think they're still out here? We saw them drive off." Jess shivered and wiped her tears with the back of her sleeve.

"One of them could have pretended to drive away and turned off their car just to fish us out. Follow me and be extremely quiet." He held tightly onto her hand and pulled her back in the direction of his pickup.

It was taking a huge chance that this wasn't a trick, but he needed to get Jess to a safer place. Guilt burned in his chest. Tom was right. If only he'd listened and taken Jess straight to the cabin. The possibility of someone seeing her near what could be the killer's house was even higher now than before. He'd broken yet another promise to her.

Michael let out a sigh of relief when they walked through the door of the cabin, but he wouldn't fully let down his guard. He would have to make a quick sweep of the house to make sure no one was there waiting for them. The front door led into a small open living room that was connected to the kitchen. There was one bedroom and a short sofa. He gave a silent groan. By the looks of the tiny couch, he wasn't going to get much sleep while they were out here. Jess followed him throughout the house as he looked behind doors and checked to make sure windows were locked.

He flipped the light on in the bedroom, took a quick scan of the room, checked the closet, then turned the light back off.

"Actually, can you leave that on?" Her voice had a quiver to it.

"Uh, sure. But stay away from the windows. I'm not taking any more chances," he said.

Michael placed the emergency duffel bag he kept in his car on the floor. It had some food, a change of clothes, and basic toiletries. Except the food, he brought wouldn't last the two of them very long. He would need to sneak back to town and get them some more supplies if this case lasted much longer.

"You can have the bedroom. I'll take the couch," he offered.

Jess stared at the bedroom door for a moment. She rubbed the back of her neck with the hand that wasn't tucked into her pocket. Her silence told him that she was still pretty shaken up. She was the strongest person he knew. But she looked like a frightened child staring into the tiny room. Her fear was completely justified, but he still hated seeing her like that.

He took a step toward her, gently touching her arm. "You okay?"

She turned to face him, tears streaming down her cheeks. "I just want my old life back."

"I'll make sure you get it." Michael wrapped his arms around her, letting his chin rest on top of her head.

"I'm so glad I ran into you that day. You saved my life," She stepped back to look him in the eyes.

"In all the chaos, I haven't said thank you," her chocolate brown doe eyes stared into his. He could feel his heart fluttering. He thought about when he'd kissed her this morning. He was just about to kiss her again when she pressed her lips to his.

"You're welcome," He whispered after she pulled away.

Without another word, she rushed into the bedroom, shutting the door behind her.

*****

Michael woke the next morning, giving his sore neck a quick massage. Maybe tonight, he'd try sleeping on the floor. His heart nearly leaped out of his chest when he discovered the bedroom door open. He peered in to see Jess lying on her side. He thought it best to let her sleep for a while longer while he made breakfast. He pulled the canned food and non-perishables out of his bag and got busy. His stomach growled as the chunky stew he'd thrown together simmered. The stew was ready to eat about twenty minutes later. He found some coffee in the cabinets and started brewing a pot.

"Morning." Jess's sleepy voice said from behind him.

He turned to see her standing next to the short, lumpy sofa.

"Hi. I didn't realize you were up. I made breakfast." Michael wiped a sweaty palm on his jeans. "I had a few things to throw together for a stew. It's not exactly bacon and eggs, but it's pretty good if I do say so myself."

"Thanks. It smells great." Jess looked stunning. Her hair was pulled back into a ponytail just like it had been the day before. Her forest green, long sleeve shirt was baggy, hanging to her mid-thigh. Her jeans were dark, and she was wearing running shoes.

She settled herself at the little two-chair table in the corner. Michael joined her, carrying two bowls of stew.

He glanced up at her as she slowly swirled a chunk of potato around in her bowl. "You really need to get something in your stomach."

"I know. I guess I'm just not hungry this morning." She said.

She looked like she didn't get much sleep. Understandably so.

"Still..." He said, wishing there was something else he could say that might make her feel a little better.

"I actually want to tell you something. About last night, I mean." She began, dropping her spoon in her bowl with a clack.

Michael stared at her, waiting for her to say what was on her mind.

"I'm sorry about the kiss. I had a lot of adrenaline running, and I was scared."

Michael's heart sank a little as she continued giving every logical explanation possible for why she kissed him. He wasn't a bit sorry for the kiss. It gave him a little ray of hope that she would forgive him for what he'd done.

"Anyway, I hope when this is over that maybe we can be friends," she finished.

He mulled her words over in his mind. Did she "just" want to be friends, or did she think he was upset with her for kissing him? He thought he'd made it clear that he still had feelings for her when he kissed her at the group home yesterday morning. She must not have gotten the message. It was in both their best interests if there wasn't any more kissing happening between them. For now.

"Are you wanting me to call a truce or something?"

"No, I don't know what I mean. I guess I'm just embarrassed. That's not how I normally act in a crisis," she explained.

"I know." He knew more about it than she realized.

CHAPTER 11

Jess had to get a few minutes away from Michael. It wasn't a good idea to go outside alone, so the only way to "get away" from him was to go into the bedroom, which was just a few feet from where he was sitting. She told him she needed to check on Tammy, but she was actually too embarrassed to be in the same room with him right now. She couldn't look at him without thinking about how gentle his kiss was. She pulled her phone from her back pocket and tapped the screen. No missed calls or texts. It was almost noon. A good time to call and see how Tammy was doing. It had been two days since the attack, and she hadn't checked on her friend once since leaving the hospital. Some friend she was. She should've called sooner.

Michael was sitting at the table in the kitchen, on the phone himself. She was pretty sure he was talking to Harry from the police station. It made her feel good to know that he had friends. She peeked out the bedroom door, studying him for a brief moment. He seemed to be listening closely to what was being said. Was there new information on the case? They seemed to be talking about a local drug ring.

Hayden, her boss, told her that there wasn't anything like that in their town and that the girls in Safe Haven were getting it from Cincinnati. Jess couldn't understand how someone as smart as Hayden could be so ignorant about such things. Michael glanced at where she stood in the doorway and smiled at her.

Darn! She didn't mean for him to catch her staring. She quickly turned and stepped out onto the porch, shutting the front door behind her. She was greeted by the cool mid-morning sunshine. She closed her eyes and took in a shaky breath, seating herself on the porch step. She wished this was some sort of relaxing vacation where she could breathe easy and go where she pleased. But it wasn't.

The woods surrounding the cabin were thick. They beckoned her. She'd give anything to take a long peaceful hike through them. But it wouldn't be peaceful at all. Not even standing on the porch was peaceful. She couldn't be sure, but it was like someone was watching her. Each beautiful tree could be a shield for a stalker.

A stream ran into a large pond about fifty yards away from where she stood. That must be where Tom went fishing when he came up here. She wondered if it was a good place for swimming. Her mind flashed again to the image of two men dressed in black hiding between the trees. Watching her. Waiting for her to step away from the cabin so they could kill her before Michael had even discovered where she was. She would have to make this quick.

Her phone in one hand, she dug in her pocket with the other, searching for the small hospital notepad with Tammy's room number scribbled on it. Should she try the phone in Tammy's room? She dialed the number and placed the phone to her ear. It wouldn't hurt anything to try it once. It rang three times before she heard a small weak voice answer.

"Hello," the voice said.

"Tammy? Is that really you?" Tears threatened to run down her cheeks.

Thank you, Lord. She may not have felt like God was watching over her, but he certainly had to be watching over Tammy for her to already be able to answer the phone.

"I'm so glad to hear your voice. How are you doing?" It was all she could do to keep from asking a million questions at once.

Tammy might remember something that would help them solve the case, or maybe she got a good look at the killer.

Judging by her voice, she had a long road to recovery ahead of her. Jess knew she'd better get her answers quick.

"Not good. But the doctors are saying I'll be alright in time." She breathed in a ragged gasp of air.

"I wanted to check on you and see if you could tell me anything you remember about who did this to you," she pressed.

"The only thing I can remember is hearing a crash. Like something was knocked over. After that, it's all black. The doctor says I might remember a little more as I recover."

"Of course." Jess tried to hide her disappointment.

"Okay. I'll let the police here know. You get some rest, and I'll come see you as soon as I can."

"Thanks, Jess," Tammy replied. The phone beeped. Jess hung up the phone and shoved it back into her pocket.

She knew Tammy's condition wasn't her fault, but still, she couldn't help but feel responsible. She might've been in her shoes right now, or Annabelle's, if not for Michael. He'd shown up at the right place, at just the right time. That brought back another one of her parents' lessons about how God worked things out for our good.

Michael had always been the knight-in-shining-armor type. Their relationship had been like a fairytale from the very beginning. Michael had transferred to their high school in his senior year, and she instantly fell in love with him. She remembered the very moment he saw her sitting in the center of the classroom. He smiled at her in the same way he smiled at her a moment ago before she came outside. The smile that rocked her world. Just like it had today.

She'd tried so hard these last few days to keep their relationship professional, but they'd already kissed twice. And Michael wasn't the only one at fault.

There was no doubt. The feelings she used to have for him were still there. She wanted to be angry that she couldn't keep herself from falling for his smile and charm, but she wasn't. She thought about her suggestion to him earlier about being friends when this was over. When he wasn't on the job, of course. He'd made it very clear to her six years ago that he didn't want to be with her. But maybe, just maybe, she could still be around him every now and then.

"Mind if I join you?" Michael suddenly appeared right behind her. She flinched.

"You just scared me out of ten years!" She crossed her arms, pretending to be mad as he sat himself on the porch step next to her.

"Harry told me they got a warrant to search that house," he informed her.

"And?"

"They didn't find anything. The house was completely cleared out, which tells me that someone must've been there, and we scared them off." His face twitched as he bit the inside of his cheek. She could almost see the wheels turning in his head.

"So what happens now?" She resisted the urge to scoot herself closer to him.

"Harry told me they found drugs in Annabelle's system. He's looking into where she may have gotten them. That's all they know so far." Michael pushed himself up off the porch step and began pacing like a caged tiger.

"I really thought he'd have more by now,"

"That doesn't make any sense. Annabelle never struggled with drugs. Of any kind. It would've been in her file if she had." Jess said.

"It was something to knock her out," Michael added.

"She knew him, then. How else could someone slip her something?" Jess blew the words out. Her stomach tightened, making the spot where she'd been punched sore.

"That's what we're thinking,"

Jess chewed her bottom lip. She wasn't sure if this case was making more sense, or less.

*****

Michael's heart was like a ticking time bomb about to explode. Anxiety had been something he battled with all his life, until he met Jess. She'd somehow always been able to make everything seem like it would be okay, even in a hopeless situation. It was one of the many things he'd missed about her since their breakup. Now here she was, back in his life. He only wished he knew how to reach out to her now for that same love and support.

"No offense. But I feel like you're better suited to handle the case than Harry is. He's a nice kid and all, but you seem to know more of what you're doing than he does," Jess pointed out.

She was right about one thing. He did know more about this case than Harry, but he wasn't about to just push him aside and take over.

"Harry's a great cop. I think he can handle himself just fine."

"I didn't mean anything by that. I just don't think you should be cooped up here protecting me." She swirled the toe of her shoe around in the dirt, making shapes.

"I don't mind. I'm following orders," Michael mumbled, watching her for a moment. A wave of warmth washed over him as he studied her ebony locks.

He'd always loved the way her dark hair made her skin look brighter like an angel. He used to call her Snow White. She *hated* it.

Michael rubbed his chin. Snow White. That gave him an idea. In the story, the wicked queen went undercover to lure Snow White out so she could kill her. What if there was a way to lure out the killer? If this case had something to do with the drug ring, then maybe sending someone in might get them more information.

He rushed back into the house and swiped his phone from the counter. He scrolled through his contact list, tapped Carl Simpson, and stuck the phone to his ear.

"Hey, Mike! Long time no see," Carl said, sarcastically.

"Funny. Can you come to Oakwood? I may have something that might help the Tammy Lenore case."

CHAPTER 12

Michael seemed a little more upbeat after his sudden phone call. Had he figured something out about the case? Jess considered asking him about it. She didn't like to be lied to or kept in the dark. Another part of her wanted to trust him. To trust his judgment. If it was necessary for her to know about it, surely Michael would have told her. She'd once trusted him wholeheartedly. She still considered those years the happiest of her life.

As the late afternoon turned into evening, Jess grew bored from sitting so long waiting for word on the case. The coolness of the evening beckoned her. She hadn't hiked much since she and Michael broke up. Would he be up to going with her, or would it remind him too much of their past and make it awkward?

She entered the cabin to find him munching on a granola bar. She had to smile at the way he tried to hide the fact that he was snacking.

"Caught you red handed," she teased.

"I was gonna let you get some sunshine for as long as you could," he replied with a boyish smirk that made him twice as adorable.

"I was thinking about going on a little hike through the woods nearby. It looks like there are a few trails, and I thought we could get some exercise." Her insides twisted.

She half expected him to make a joke or say no, but instead, his eyes brightened a little at the idea.

"I'd love to, but it might not be such a good idea. The killer could've tracked us here." he pointed out.

"We don't know that they did. And if they have, maybe we can catch them and close this case ourselves." At this point, she was willing to do whatever it took to feel free again.

Michael stared at her for a moment.

"Well?" she pushed.

"Ok, but we run back here at the first sign of trouble,"

"Agreed." Jess hurried into the bedroom, grabbing a water bottle from her bag and nearly sprinting for the backdoor.

Michael followed closely at her heels. "Slow down."

There wasn't a porch on the back of the cabin like there was on the front. Just a few small stone steps. There was a big open field behind the cabin with a tree line about a quarter-mile away. It was nothing for her and Michael to walk five miles or more back when they were together.

He quickly caught up to her. It felt as if she had been transported back in time. She and Michael were hiking alone in the woods just like they used to. She was happy then and so much in love with him. But then he'd vanished from her life. He abandoned her. She wouldn't have guessed in a million years that she'd be doing this with him again.

Abandoned. That was a word she'd tried to keep at bay, but if she was really honest with herself, it's how she truly felt.

"So, what happened between you and Tiffany? You guys seemed happy the last time I saw you." Even though it was a question that had been burning in her mind from the moment he stepped back into her life, she still couldn't help the uncomfortable feeling that twisted her stomach into knots. She half expected him to quickly change the subject.

"This isn't something I normally like to talk about. But I think I owe it to you to tell you. Tiffany was sort of a rebound after you and I...you know. She didn't think of herself that way, though. She thought we were meant to be together. It wasn't long after we got married that I learned who she really was. She started hitting me and kicking me whenever she got upset." Michael's voice changed a little when he started talking about Tiffany's abuse. As if he was re-living it.

Jess's heart shattered into a million pieces. She couldn't help but feel like she was partially to blame.

"That's awful," she whispered. It was all she could think to say.

It was easy to look at a woman in an abusive relationship and want to help her escape. There were even lots of resources to help women get out of those situations. But men. It was a hard concept to grasp.

"I would never hit a woman. She knew that, and she used it to her advantage. Then, one day, she met someone new and left. I think she found out she was no match for you."

His last few words caught in Jess's ear. It sounded as if he still had feelings for her. Or was that just something she wanted to hear? She tried to think of something to say to ignore the implication he'd made. She wanted to tell him that she'd never fully gotten over him either, but after what he'd gone through, she was sure that was the last thing he wanted to hear. She now understood the rustic cabin. The seclusion. He needed time to heal.

"I can't imagine how you must feel," she finally said. "I deal with abused women all the time. I try to tell them to watch out for men who try to be like knights in shining armor. Kind of like Hayden Cunningham. My boss. I've seen him flirt with a few of the girls. Nothing really serious, but still really inappropriate. He got a slap on the wrist. That's all. Guys like him like to prey on vulnerable women."

"How does he try to act like a knight in shining armor?" Michael sounded concerned.

"He's gone to Safe Haven a few times. We're not supposed to know. But I've heard he's secretly dated a few of the women that have come through," Jess explained.

Michael stopped not far behind her, pushing a tree branch out of his way. "Why aren't you supposed to know? If he's your boss, he should be allowed on the premises, right?"

"His job is in the office. He mostly runs the books and writes the paychecks. Only certain people are allowed inside. Attorneys, counselors, social workers, people like that," She explained.

"Do you know of any time he's come to Safe Haven recently?" Michael asked. Jess also stopped, turning to face him.

"Yes, now that you mention it. He went there about two weeks ago. He never said what for. Why do you ask?"

His face turned to a frown as his gaze drifted to the ground. The evening grew muggy, and mosquitoes buzzed around their sweaty faces.

"Michael?"

"Based on what you just said, Hayden Cunningham is another male who had access to Annabelle prior to her moving back home. Which means he's now very high on our suspect list."

Jess had never considered that her own boss would kill anyone. He wasn't a very likable person, but was he the type that would take someone's life? She doubted it.

"We need to head back. I need to call Harry again and tell him what you said about your boss." Michael turned and hurried back the way they came. She didn't want to be cooped up in the cabin again, but he was right. They needed to explore every possibility if they were going to find out who killed Annabelle and who was trying to kill her.

She'd wanted to get out into nature and enjoy it, but after hearing about his horrible marriage to her ex-best friend, she couldn't think about enjoying anything.

*****

Michael could barely see his hand in front of his face by the time they got back to the cabin. He never should've let Jess convince him to go on a hike with her. She didn't know it, but her ponytail swaying with every step and her big brown eyes staring back at him was very distracting.

He'd allowed them to be put in a vulnerable position that might've cost both of them their lives. Michael pushed massive branches out of his face causing them to creak. There was a trail here, just like Jess had said, but he should've known to head back earlier so they could find their way before it got dark.

They finally came to the clearing behind the cabin after several minutes. Michael gave an inward sigh of relief. He stepped aside and let Jess walk in front of him. She marched in and flipped the light on. He could see the disappointment on her face. She'd always loved the hiking trips they used to take. Maybe when this case was solved, he could ask her out for another hiking trip.

No, he couldn't think that way. He was a police officer for the Oakwood Springs P.D., and he was protecting a witness in a murder investigation. He really needed to get his head in the game. Too many times, he'd gotten careless. Yes, Jess still meant a lot to him. But he had to remember that he was on the job and should act like it.

"I'm going to call the hospital again and see how Tammy's doing." Jess waved her cellphone at him.

He nodded in approval and picked up his phone to dial Harry again.

"What's up, Mike?" Harry's voice said on the other end of the line.

"Things are pretty quiet here, but I think I've got some info that might be important to the case," Michael told Harry about Hayden Cunningham visiting the group home and secretly dating a few of the women.

The idea angered him. These women were in a delicate state, and to take advantage of that state was beyond wrong.

"Hmm. Looks like he fits the profile pretty well," Harry commented.

"Check into him, will ya? See if he has an alibi for the time of Annabelle Mason's murder too."

"Sure thing," Harry replied, then hung up.

Michael placed his phone back on the counter where it had been charging all day. He wasn't sure how long Jess would take in the other room, so he thought he'd better have a hot meal waiting for her when she was finished. He opened the freezer door and found two steaks.

"Steak and potatoes it is."

Before long, the kitchen smelled of the delicious aroma of seared steak and buttery potatoes. Just before the potatoes were finished cooking, Jess came out of the bedroom. Her eyes were red, and she was trying to quickly wipe away tears before he could notice.

"Have I died and gone to heaven? This smells absolutely delicious." She set her phone on the counter next to his and plopped down at the table.

He smiled at the praise.

"When did you learn to cook like this? We're in a cabin in the middle of nowhere with someone trying to kill us, and you're making gourmet food that should be served in a five-star restaurant." She closed her eyes and inhaled deeply.

"Things don't have to be all bad right now." Michael felt like he was doing her job. She was usually the one who did her best to brighten everyone's day.

"I'm going back to town in the morning. We need some supplies, but I'm going to check on a few things that might help solve this case a little quicker," he announced as he set the plates on the table and seated himself across from her. She took a big bite of the steak, staring at him as she chewed. He scooped up some potatoes and placed them on her plate.

"You think that's a good idea after the incident on the way here," she said after swallowing. Her eyes met his.

"Maybe not. But I have more connections in Cincinnati than Tom does, and I intend to use them," he said.

"I would like to check on things at my apartment, and I wouldn't mind getting a better blend of coffee. The cup I had this morning tasted a lot like mud." She said.

"That's the part you aren't going to like," he added. He knew Jess too well. She wasn't one to be told no.

"What do you mean?" She crossed her arms.

"You aren't coming. There's no way I'm going to bring you back to town with me so the killer can make another attempt on your life."

Jess opened her mouth to protest but stopped herself.

"I just don't want anything to happen to you. In fact, nothing has happened since we've been here. You're safe here, and I'll only be gone for an hour or two." He continued.

"I'd argue with you on that if you weren't right. But my brain is going to melt if I stay in this cabin much longer," she said.

"Your safety is the most important thing right now, and I'm sure your brain can take being here a little longer." He waited for her to protest further, but she didn't. Couldn't she see that he was willing to sacrifice everything for her?

Just as Jess stood to carry her plate to the sink, her phone vibrated. She sat her plate down on the dark green countertop next to the sink and picked it up. Her brow dropped into a frown.

"It's Hayden." Her tone told him that she was confused at the fact that he was calling her.

He personally didn't know any boss that would call their employees this late in the evening.

"What's up, Hayden?" She tried to sound upbeat as she slipped into the bedroom to finish her conversation, her voice trailing away until he could no longer hear what she was saying. Part of him wished he could listen in on the conversation. There wasn't any direct evidence pointing to Hayden. But it was getting harder for him to control the desperation to solve this case. He sighed, hoping to calm the anxiety tingling in his chest. At least Hayden didn't know their location. Even if he wasn't the killer, they couldn't take any chances.

CHAPTER 13

Jess awoke to a knock at the bedroom door. It couldn't be morning already. A small stream of light coming from between the curtains told her that it was. She climbed out of bed, then noticed she was wearing the same clothes from last night. She quickly changed and ran her fingers through her hair to smooth it down.

When she entered the living room, Michael was rummaging through his duffel bag. She noted the red and black flannel shirt he was wearing. It looked identical to a shirt she'd gotten him the Christmas before they broke up. Could it be the same one?

"Did you sleep well?" He asked, zipping up the duffel bag.

"As well as anyone in witness protection could," she said with a shrug. She watched him pull a glock out of the side pocket. He handed it to her.

"Don't be afraid to use this, if necessary," he said. Her hand wrapped around the grip. She'd never fired a gun. The thought of having to fire it terrified her, yet she felt better about having it. It tempted her to get a pistol of her own when this was over.

Michael turned around and zipped the duffel bag back up. As he turned, she noticed the outline of another pistol holstered on his hip, pressing through the flannel.

"You never said why Hayden called last night." Michael pointed out. She pressed her lips together. She never came out of the bedroom after that call. Keeping her distance from him as much as possible would be the only way to make it through this without making a fool of herself.

"He acted really strange."

"How so?" He stopped and gave her his full attention.

"He kept asking me where the police had me staying and if there was anything he could bring me. That's not like him. He's never been the concerned type." She couldn't think of one instance where he called her, Marge, or anyone else she worked with to see if they needed anything.

I'll tell Harry to keep a closer eye on him. Just stay inside and keep the doors locked and I'll be back in an hour," he said.

His instructions made her feel like she was thirteen again when her parents would leave her home alone.

Michael opened the front door to reveal a bright sunny morning. Normally she would be happy about that, but she couldn't enjoy it with a killer on the loose. Maybe she could take a short run and be back before he knew she'd gone anywhere.

Before she knew it, his truck disappeared in the distance. If he felt she was safe enough out here by herself, then surely it was alright to take a quick run. There wasn't a TV or any books here. She'd go crazy if she had to stay cooped up inside all day.

Jess laced up her running shoes while sitting on the steps of the front porch. The air was warm and held a hint of honeysuckle and cool Ohio dirt. The nightmare of the last few days seemed to be driven away by the sunshine. Summer was on its way fast, and she was ready for the warm weather. She stood, checking her pocket for her phone, then adjusted the belt around her middle containing the pistol and holster that Michael gave her. This run was to help her relax a little and clear her head, but it was still a good idea to be prepared, just in case. She would only go about a mile, then back. That wouldn't be too dangerous, right? She figured the only thing she'd have to worry about around here was an animal.

She trotted about a hundred yards from the cabin. Warming up was one of her favorite parts. It was as if her body was building up the anticipation of something wonderful. As she came upon a field peppered with yellow and purple flowers, she noticed something moving between the bushes. Her heart fluttered.

Calm down. It's just a rabbit or something. You're safe here. She ran a little faster, trying to force herself to enjoy what a beautiful day it was. But she couldn't. Something tugged at her mind. She'd had the feeling of being watched before, but this time it was stronger. She turned and glanced over her shoulder. The cabin was now out of sight. She figured she was about a quarter-mile away from it.

The woods behind her ran parallel to the road. Maybe she could cut through there. She'd be back inside the cabin in half the time. She should've listened to Michael.

Going crazy from boredom was better than ending up dead in the woods.

Jess looked back over the field where she thought she saw a rabbit cutting through the bushes. Something black moved just inside the tree line. She was being watched. The sound of her pounding heart in her ears was deafening. She slowed herself to a stop and pretended to stretch. If she gave any indication that she knew someone was out there, she could be done for. Her best chance was to act natural and try to casually make her way back. She turned and trotted back the way she came. She tried to calculate in her mind how much farther the cabin was.

Jess could feel the presence of someone following her down the gravel road. She took a quick peek behind her. A figure dressed in black with a mask covering their nose and mouth was quickly slinking toward her. She recognized the baseball cap he had on. It was just like the man she'd seen at Annabelle's. He had her.

Jess took off running. She had to make it back to the cabin. Why didn't she listen to Michael? The gun. Would she have time to get it out of the holster? Her hand went to her side and gripped the handle. She had no experience with weapons. She hadn't needed it. She'd worked so many cases where a woman with no shooting experience tried to defend herself but instead had a pistol ripped from her hand. Each case went through her mind like an assembly line.

The footsteps behind her grew louder, telling her that he was getting closer. Jess ducked into the woods. Taking the shortcut was her best chance of survival. She leaped over a small fallen tree and ducked to avoid a low-hanging branch from another tree. Her lungs began to burn. This was not the sort of running she had in mind.

She let out a gasp when the cabin came into view. She just might make it. If she could just get through the door and lock it behind her, she'd be safe just long enough to call Michael and tell him that the killer was after her. Her heart pounded faster. She had no idea if she'd lost the dark figure or if he was just inches away from grabbing her. All she could hear was the sound of her own heavy breathing.

Each breath sent a fire-like pain shooting through her chest. She made a huge leap onto the porch. Her foot pressed into the floor of the cabin to slow herself enough to slam the door behind her and lock it. *Yes.* She'd made it.

Her hands shook as she fumbled her phone out of her pocket, dropping the pistol on the couch cushion just as the black shadow began pounding on the door. She scrambled through her list of phone numbers trying to find Michael's. She would've called 911 any other time, but he would get to her a lot quicker.

She was just about to put the phone to her ear when she heard footsteps walk up behind her. She froze. There was someone else in the house. Then she heard a loud noise as pain shot through her head. The world went black.

*****

Michael took in a deep breath before walking into the Oakwood Springs Police Station. Tom would reprimand him and possibly fire him for being here, but he was willing to take that risk to help Jess. His orders were to protect her, but he needed to get some answers. Nothing was making sense. He was supposed to be getting some supplies, but Oakwood Springs had one grocery store, and it happened to be next door to the OSPD. Stopping in for a quick update on the case wouldn't hurt anything.

He'd be in and out before Tom even knew he'd been here. He entered, smelling the all-too-familiar fragrance of burnt coffee, recycled paper, and hard work. He walked past the front desk and down the hall to where he knew Harry would be. Sure enough, he was at his desk, staring at a computer screen.

Harry's eyes flickered with surprise when he caught sight of him. "You really shouldn't be here. Where's the witness?"

"And you really should be out on patrol. The witness is in a safe place. Are there any new developments in the case that I don't know about?" Michael shot back.

Harry rummaged through the stack of papers and folders on his desk. "Yeah. I have a report here. Hayden Cunningham has an alibi for the day of Annabelle Mason's murder."

"Which is?" Michael twirled his hand, gesturing for Harry to continue.

"The murder took place around 3:45 p.m. Cunningham claims he was at lunch on the day of the murder at a little place called Sam's Deli. He showed us a receipt marked for the day and time of the murder."

Michael frowned. "Were you able to find any indication of his involvement?"

"None. Tom said for me to focus on Annabelle's father. But I haven't been able to locate him yet. He's out right now seeing if he can track anything down about local drug dealers going around the group home."

Michael was glad that at least one suspect was off their list, but he still would be doing more checking of his own.

"Thanks, Harold." He gave him a firm slap on the back.

"Very funny. You might want to sneak out the back so you don't run into Tom," Harry warned.

"I think I can handle Tom." Michael stiffened, putting forward his best tough-guy persona. It was just a show. No one here ever needed to 'handle' Tom. He was understanding. Well, most of the time, he was. He was grateful to Tom for giving him a chance here when he moved to Oakwood Springs, and he respected him a great deal. He never disobeyed orders unless he absolutely had to. Getting supplies was a must. Having an update to bring back to Jess was not. He just wanted to put her mind at ease. At least a little bit. Maybe tonight, he'd make her his special seafood chowder. He stopped that thought in its tracks. This wasn't one of the romantic getaways they used to take. Why was he still trying to be her hero?

Yes, this was the only woman he ever loved. The woman who'd had his heart since high school and still did if he was totally honest with himself. But that ship had sailed.

Michael hurried back to his car, giving a glance over his shoulder every moment or two to make sure Tom didn't spot him. He was obviously very protective of Jess like a father would be over a daughter. But he knew Jess a lot better than Tom did and knew she was pretty good at taking care of herself. Still, a little pang of concern wormed its way into his gut.

Yes, he'd broken one of the most important rules in the book. Never leave a witness under police protection alone. It was a huge risk, one he never took unless he absolutely had to. That was the situation in this case. He *had* to figure this out for Jess.

There really wasn't anyone he trusted 100% to handle this case. Not because he doubted their abilities as an officer of the law. This case had gotten personal. Harry was still somewhat green, and Tom would often prefer to not bring in outside help for more serious cases. He wasn't sure if it was because Tom didn't like to be outranked or because he didn't take it as seriously as others would. Whatever the reason, Michael felt like he needed to get more deeply involved. For Jess. Of course, Tom did offer his cabin as a safe house, but she couldn't stay out there forever.

The trip to the grocery store for supplies took about twenty minutes. Mostly canned goods, a loaf of bread, and a few containers of meat cluttered the bottom of his shopping cart. There was one more thing he was supposed to get. Oh yeah, Jess's coffee. She wanted a better blend than the off-brand Tom left there. He decided to get his favorite brand for her to try. Community Coffee. Medium Roast. He couldn't wait to see her face when she tasted to smooth blend he'd first fallen in love with just last year.

After he paid for the items and quickly loaded them into his truck, he climbed into the driver's seat. Just one more stop before heading back to Jess.

Carl Simpson was supposed to meet him east of town at the old, abandoned McDonald's building. Michael didn't expect him to have made a lot of progress in the last twenty-four hours, but even the smallest detail could be helpful. One small piece to the puzzle could pull it all together.

He noticed Carl's blue Camaro parked sideways across three spaces when the old McDonald's came into view. Michael turned the steering wheel sharply, gliding into the parking lot. As his pickup stopped, Carl climbed out of his car.

"Glad to see you're still in one piece," he quipped as Michael climbed out of his truck.

"Yeah, this is a pretty crazy case so far." He didn't want to give him too much info about everything that had happened since he'd last seen him. Carl had been a co-worker while he was married to Tiffany. He knew a lot about how the marriage was going and what Tiffany was like. A little more than Michael was comfortable with.

"Were you able to find anything of value?" Michael asked.

"Not much. The only thing I was able to dig up was that any drugs coming into Oakwood Springs go through one person and one person only. This is his territory, and nobody wants to mess with the guy," Carl explained.

He couldn't help but feel nostalgic about working with Carl again. He was the only good thing about working with the Cincinnati Police Department.

"Nothing that will help me solve this murder." Michael didn't even make an attempt to hide his disappointment.

"Sorry. I'll keep looking. In fact, I told the Chief I came here to look for a suspect. Since these cases could be related, I can help out a little if you need." Carl offered.

Being a detective, Carl had the authority to call shots Michael couldn't. He would have to check in with Tom, letting him know he was in town working on another case.

"I may have something that will help your investigation." Michael held up the card from Jess's apartment that Tammy Lenore sent.

Carl took the card from Michael and read it. "I don't see how this will help us." He gave Michael a skeptical look.

"That was on Jess Everett's fridge. Kind of a good indication of where she'd go if she left town."

It was a long shot, but it was the only connection they had between the two cases. But was it enough to keep Carl's expertise in Oakwood Springs? Possibly.

"So you're saying that the perp in your case went to Jess's apartment, saw this on her fridge, rushed down to Cincinnati, looked her up, then attempted to kill her to get to Jess?" Carl rubbed his chin. "That's a pretty big leap, Mike, you gotta admit."

"I think he went there looking for her," Michael said.

"That might be true. But until we have more to go on, we have to stick to facts instead of assumptions." Carl waved his hand in a "stop" gesture.

Michael let out a sigh of frustration. Carl huffed as well.

"I'll check in for old time's sake, but it's a very long shot and probably won't amount to anything." Carl slipped the card into his pocket.

"Thanks. Just remember when you check in with the sheriff to not mention you saw me." Michael added.

Carl looked confused but nodded in agreement as he climbed back into his car. "I'll let you know as soon as I figure out anything else."

Michael waved goodbye as Carl revved the engine, circled the parking lot then turned back onto the main highway.

Show off.

The morning had turned to afternoon before he realized it. He told Jess he'd only be an hour or so. He'd need to hurry and get back before it got too late.

He picked up his phone, dialed Jess, then pulled out of the parking lot.

No answer. Michael's heart fluttered with concern. He called her a second time. Nothing. Michael stomped on the gas pedal. Something was wrong. His face heated at the thought of anyone hurting her.

On the outskirts of town, he pressed the accelerator to the floor. The roar of the engine grew louder. The heaviness of his truck sent him leaning back and forth around each curve of the winding back roads. What if something had happened to her? He'd only just gotten her back in his life. He couldn't lose her now.

Everything was passing by in a blur. He needed to get to her. He was only about a mile and a half from the cabin when the thought he tried his best to avoid filled his mind. What if she was dead? No, he couldn't think like that.

Please God, let her be alive. After his quick prayer, he pushed that thought out of his mind and tried to think of all the other reasons she wasn't answering her phone. Maybe she was in the shower, or her phone was dead. She might have wanted to go on another hike and simply left her phone at the cabin.

His heart began to feel like it would pound right out of his chest when the cabin finally came into view. The bright blue sky that shrouded the little clearing when he left this morning was now darker from the misty clouds. There was no indication that Jess was outside. He slammed on the brakes, sliding to a stop on the dirt directly in front of the cabin.

His heart nearly stopped when he saw the front door was left open. An alarm went off in his head.

No. He ran around the back of his truck and leaped onto the porch, calling her name as loud as he could.

The lights were off inside the cabin. He began flipping them on as he checked the bedroom and the bathroom for her. The house was silent. Where could she have gone? He dashed for the back door. It was locked, just like it had been this morning. A faint groan came from the kitchen. Michael hurried in to find Jess's limp body on the floor. Just as he was about to grab her arm and help her up, he felt something strike the back of his head. He grabbed the spot as he dropped to his knees. How could he have let himself walk into a trap?

CHAPTER 14

Jess felt a terrible pain in the back of her head. When her eyes opened, all she could make out were shapes and colors. She squeezed her eyes shut, then reopened them, hoping that would clear her vision. She couldn't be dead because, from what she could tell, she was still in the cabin.

She rubbed the goose egg on her head as her vision started to clear. She was sitting upright on the floor in the kitchen. Her cell phone lay on the floor beside her. Hidden by the edge of the couch. They would've taken it if they'd seen it. Her mind flashed to the dark figure chasing her. Why hadn't they killed her? Her head hurt far too much to try to solve that complex puzzle right now. Jess scanned the room, fearing that the killer could still be close by. Waiting.

She'd watched a true-crime documentary a few weeks ago and heard that some killers liked their prey to be conscious. It was more satisfying for them psychologically or something spooky like that. The thought made her shiver. She'd come so close to death; she could almost touch it. The icy feeling it left in her stomach was something she never wanted to feel again.   Jess felt the need to do another quick scan of the room, just to make sure she was alone. Some of the lights had been turned on. Had she done that? She had no recollection of it. She stumbled to her feet, tightly gripping her phone so she wouldn't drop it. A wave of dizziness washed over her. She had no idea if someone was watching her from somewhere in the house. But if they were, she would need to be ready.

There was an orange hue on the wall. Sunset. Where was Michael? He should've been back hours ago. This probably wouldn't have happened if he'd been here. A heavy feeling settled over her. Maybe he wasn't coming back at all. He dropped her off out here and abandoned her. He. Abandoned. Her. Again. But he promised to protect her. She should've seen this coming. Anger started bubbling in her stomach as her mind raced through all the possibilities of why he wasn't back.

She could have been lying on the floor in a pool of her own blood. The terrible image of Annabelle gasping for her last breath sent hot tears down Jess's face. That would be her fate too, if she let down her guard with someone that couldn't be trusted. But she wanted to trust him. She wanted to be with him. To her, that was the most confusing part of the entire situation.

Jess slowly made her way to the couch. Her legs wobbled and felt tingly. The room started to spin. Maybe she was hurt worse than she'd first thought. She took another step, trying not to completely lose her balance, and end up with another bump on the head. She was going to have a tough time explaining this to Tom.

She was even angrier with herself than with Michael, even after how he treated her six years ago. She'd allowed herself to be charmed by him once again. She focused on her phone screen. Tom wouldn't have a problem coming out here to get her. She tapped the screen, causing it to light up, then opened her contacts list. Tom was saved to her favorites. She was just about to press the button to call him when something stopped her.

Compassion. Things hadn't exactly been easy for Michael either since their breakup. She always pictured him and Tiffany living happily ever after. But it wasn't anything like that. Just thinking about how she treated Michael made her want to cry and tear her former friend's arm off and beat her with it.

Jess never understood women like Tiffany. She knew Michael was a good man, which was why she thought he was worth stabbing her "best friend" in the back. But Michael had always been the gentleman type. He always paid for dinner, he opened doors, and he would never hit a woman. Not even if she hit *him.* She couldn't fathom why some women took advantage of that.

Jess took a deep breath, gripping the back of the couch tightly. Her head was still spinning. She could almost feel the blood rushing back to her legs. She took a few more deep breaths. It took about five minutes before her head felt anywhere close to normal.

Dizziness still threatened her with a fall. She took a step back toward the kitchen. She reached a hand out to grab the door frame, but before she could, her foot hit something. Jess let out a gasp. She looked down to see Michael lying on the floor, pushed up against the wall with blood coming from the back of his head. How had she not seen him there earlier?

"*No!*" She fumbled with her phone, tapping Tom's name with a shaky finger.

The room spun harder as she dropped to her knees beside him. What if he was dead? It would be all her fault. She heard Tom's voice.

"Jess? Is everythi—?"

"Tom! Tom! Come quick!" She cried.

"It's Michael. He's hurt. I think he's...." Before she could say that terrible word, she heard a soft moan come from Michael. She let out a sob of relief.

"He's alive. Thank you, God. We need help out here." She tried to stop the tears long enough to give Tom a few quick details about what had happened.

"I'll be there with an ambulance as fast as possible." She heard his keys rattle as he hung up the phone.

"Michael, can you hear me?" She shook him.

"Please don't shout." He gingerly prodded the back of his head.

She placed her hand on top of his, ignoring the warm tingle in her fingers. "Careful, you're bleeding."

He pulled his hand out from under hers and took a quick look at the red stains.

He winced. "It looks that way."

Jess felt a bit relieved that he hadn't lost his sarcastic humor. She wished her head would stop spinning so she could go and get a towel to put on the back of his head until the ambulance arrived.

It was about twenty minutes later when red and blue flashing lights filled the room. From what she could see, sitting on the floor next to Michael, there were two police cars and one ambulance. Tom burst into the room, quickly catching sight of her and Michael sitting on the floor.

He rushed over to them with Harry at his heels. The two policemen helped her and Michael to their feet and guided them to the couch. Her head hurt worse than it ever had before, and standing had caused a wave of nausea to rush over her.

"Are you alright?" Michael asked her.

"I'm not sure. I'm more worried about you than myself." She felt dizzy and nauseous. But his injury looked like it might be a lot worse than hers.

His dark hair was wet from sweat but mostly from blood. Harry went around the room, flipping on the rest of the lights. Michael squinted and held his hand in front of his face.

She knew just how he felt. The light seemed to make her headache much worse. She closed her eyes, knowing the EMTs would need the light to examine them.

"You two are lucky to be alive." Tom's voice boomed in her head.

She tried to ignore it. Both she and Michael would have to give Tom a detailed account of what they saw and remembered.

"I don't feel so lucky." She glanced over at Michael to see a blonde woman wearing a blue uniform, and bright blue latex gloves tilt his head forward and place a gauze pack on the back of his head.

She wondered if her injuries were as bad as his. A second EMT came to her and asked her the same questions she'd heard Michael answer. She tilted her head forward.

"Looks like whoever did this wasn't as angry at you as they were your friend. Yours should be gone in about a week." The EMT said. Jess felt a little relieved.

"Do either of you remember anything that might help us figure out who did this?" Tom asked.

"I went for a run this morning, and someone dressed in all black came out of the woods and chased me. I got back inside, and that's the last thing I remember." She cast a guilty glance at Michael.

He gritted his teeth and shook his head. She wanted to not care what he thought about her breaking her promise to stay inside. But she knew he was right, and not listening to his instructions nearly cost her her life.

"And where were you when this was going on?" Tom's tone went from concerned to angry when he turned his attention to Michael.

"Out," was Michael's response.

"You're gonna have to do better than that." Tom was growing angrier by the second. His face went from a tan to a bright red.

She couldn't tell if it was because she'd gotten hurt or because there was something Michael wasn't telling him.

Jess didn't want things to grow worse... or louder for that matter. "Can we have a quieter conversation, please? My head is killing me."

The room fell silent for a moment. She looked over to see the blonde woman stitching up Michael's head. He sucked in a breath through his teeth.

"So he's alright?" She tried not to sound too concerned. She didn't want anyone getting the wrong idea about her and Michael.

"Oh yeah, whatever hit him just so happened to cut into the skin. It looks worse than it is. A few stitches to help close the wound and some antibiotics, and he should be okay. But he'll need to come to the clinic to have it checked in a day or two just to make sure my stitches are holding up," The EMT explained.

Jess thanked her.

"You're welcome. Normally we would be taking you both back to the clinic to run some tests to make sure neither of you has a concussion and would need to be transported to the Cincinnati Hospital. But we got orders not to."

A few minutes later, The two ambulances drove off in a hurry with their lights flashing. Jess stood in the doorway, catching a breath of fresh air. She frowned in confusion. Wasn't that the procedure for when there was a patient in need of immediate attention?

Tom appeared at her side. "That should buy us just enough time to regroup and make a new plan. If the killer is still close by, they'll think you and Michael are being rushed to the hospital," he explained.

He led her back to the couch, and she settled next to Michael once again.

"This attack confuses me the more I think about it. It's different from the other attacks." Tom paced in front of them in the living room.

"Yeah, we're both still alive," Michael quipped.

"That's the question of the hour right now," Harry chimed in from the kitchen.

Jess shook her head. She hadn't remembered that he was here. He walked into the living room carrying a small tray with four steamy cups of coffee. Jess grabbed one and took a quick sip. The warmth in her mouth and throat eased her headache.

Michael picked up a cup as well. "If this person was the killer, we'd both be dead right now."

Jess hadn't thought of the possibility of whoever was chasing her not being the killer.

"If this wasn't the killer, then who was it, and why would they do this?" She rubbed the back of her head.

"Maybe they were going to kill you, but something scared them off," Harry suggested.

"What I don't understand is why they waited to hit me over the head as well," Michael said.

Jess was growing overwhelmed by all of their suggestions. She tried to work up an image in her mind of the person chasing her. Their frame seemed smaller than the man who chased her on the day of Annabelle's murder. Being chased by a killer and a potential killer in less than a week was enough to cause anyone to lose their mind. And she wasn't far from it.

She wrapped her arms around herself. Even though she was surrounded by police officers, she still felt alone and scared. Her body was tired and sore, but there was no way she would be able to sleep tonight.

"Are you doing okay?" Michael slid across the couch, so close that his hip was almost up against her leg.

"No. But I'll be a little better once I drink this coffee." She took another sip from the warm mug and glanced at Tom, who noticed Michael's concern.

"Since this case is growing more dangerous, I think another officer should stay out here to protect Jess. Especially since you're injured and may have a concussion." Tom explained.

Jess was glad that Tom got Michael's attention off her. The warmth that crept into her cheeks when he spoke to her was something she wasn't ready to feel.

"I'll be more than happy to stay." Harry beamed at Michael. His tone was almost pleading.

Jess remembered what Michael said about taking Harry under his wing on the job. She could see the admiration for him in Harry's eyes. Almost like a little brother looking for the approval of an older sibling.

"I think I should be the one to stay here tonight," Tom offered.

Jess noted the disappointment on Harry's face.

"I don't think that's a good idea. You'll be needed in town more than you're needed here," Michael said.

Tom gave him a look that told Jess he didn't like that response. The tension between the two men was only getting worse. What bothered her was that the killer got the drop on Michael. If the killer came back, would two officers be enough?

*****

Michael tried to hide the fact that his head was throbbing. His boss was sitting right in front of him, and he didn't want to be taken off the case. The pain hovering on the back of his head was just beginning to dull. He figured the medication he'd received earlier was starting to kick in.

He didn't deserve pain meds. This whole situation was his fault. He never should've left Jess alone. He stole a glance her way. There weren't any visible signs that she'd been hit on the head at all. Guilt was ripping his insides to shreds.

"I think we should set a trap for this guy, and I think I know how to do that," Jess said.

"How?" Michael responded.

"If I let it be known that I've gone home. The killer obviously knows where I live, and you—" He held up his hand, stopping her right there.

"No way. That's far too risky.".

"That isn't a half-bad plan," Tom chimed in.

A red hot bubble of rage grew in Michael's chest. How could he think of putting her in danger that way? He was supposed to care about her.

"What if she gets hurt?" Michael didn't usually challenge Tom, but what they were suggesting was a risk he didn't want to take.

"We'll have half a dozen officers close by. She can signal us when the perp is close enough to nab," Tom said.

Michael rocked to his feet. The room wobbled in his view, but he ignored it. He was the cause of her being injured today. A huge mistake. He wasn't about to be part of anything that put her in danger again. He circled the chair where Harry was sitting and started for the door. He needed the cool night air on his sweating forehead.

Just as he was about to exit the cabin, a white spot on the floor caught his eye. He suddenly stopped, leaned down, and picked it up—it felt like a sliver of paper. He unfolded it, discovering it was a receipt from Sam's Deli. He read the date and time printed across the top. Flipping it over, he found some light scribbles written in pencil on the back.

12 p.m. Take care of them both.

"Did one of you guys drop this?" Michael rejoined the group and returned to the spot he'd occupied earlier. He held out the receipt.

Tom grabbed it, closely reading the name printed across the top. "No, this isn't mine. I don't really care for that place."

"Me neither." Harry took a peek at the small strip of paper over Tom's shoulder.

Jess took it from Tom's hand. "You don't suppose this was dropped by the person who attacked us, do you?" She sounded hopeful, more hopeful than she should've.

"One of the EMTs could have dropped it," Tom quickly answered.

"I think 'Take care of them both' isn't something an EMT would need to write down and keep in their pocket," Michael said.

"12 p.m. was around the time I was out running today." Fear crept into Jess's voice.

"It looks to me like this was premeditated. But I'm not sure it was done by the killer," Michael said.

"Since I'm on my way back to town, I'll call Sam's Deli and see if I can get surveillance footage so we can figure out who made this purchase. Who knows? Maybe Sam will remember what the guy looked like." Tom stood with a groan.

"You call me if there's any more trouble," he said to Jess. He gave Michael a burning glance.

If looks could kill.

"Or if you're left alone again," He added. Jess nodded in response.

Slowly, the blue flashing lights of Tom's cruiser disappeared out of sight. The cabin grew quiet. He should try to get some sleep... or at least give it a shot. He didn't imagine anything else happening tonight, but if it did, he was glad he had Harry here for backup.

CHAPTER 15

As Jess entered the bedroom, she felt seconds away from falling asleep. A good night's sleep. That was just what she needed after the horrible, frightening, nightmare-inducing week she'd had. She allowed herself to fall back on the bed. She didn't have the strength to change out of her clothes. She kicked her shoes off, then crawled under the protection of the comforter. She said a quick prayer for Tom—that he would make it home alright and that he would be able to learn something from the clue Michael had discovered on the floor.

Tom had promised her just before he left that he would get the information on who made the purchase from Sam's Deli. They would finally have something to go on. The memory of the killer's large form standing behind her would have her looking over her shoulder for the rest of her life. Not even catching the guy would make that feeling go away. Still, if this clue led to them catching him, maybe she could get some kind of closure. More importantly, they would get justice for Annabelle and for Tammy.

Tammy. She needed to check on her. Jess hoped she would remember enough to give the police a detailed description of who attacked her.

Lord willing. Her mother used that phrase a lot when she was younger. God's will was something difficult to understand right now. She didn't know how to feel, really. Should she be angry at God for allowing her life to turn into a complete mess, or should she be thankful that she still had life? It was an overwhelming concept. One that caused her head to hurt worse. No, better keep it simple. They would be one step closer to learning who brutally murdered Annabelle and had her in his sights to silence her.

Jess took long deep breaths, trying to allow her mind to relax. Her body felt like it was melting into a puddle on the old spring mattress. She knew she could rest easy with Harry and Michael in the other room but still found it difficult.

*****

Michael quickly sat up on the couch. He rubbed the back of his head in an attempt to massage away the soreness from sleeping on the lumpy couch pillow. He heard a buzzing sound coming from where he'd laid his phone. Picking it up, he read Sherriff Tom's name across the screen. He reluctantly swiped the screen to answer.

"Morning, Sherriff."

"Good morning. How's our witness?" He sounded as if he was on a mission.

"She isn't awake yet," Michael wanted to end the call right there and go back to sleep.

Tom's husky voice was causing the soreness in his head to grow worse. "I thought I'd let you know that I went into Sam's Deli this morning and checked into that receipt you found."

"And?"

"Turns out that particular person was Hayden Cunningham. It was paid for with a credit card," Tom informed him.

Michael remembered the suspicious looking man sitting in the back of the deli. And that he wasn't alone.

"I think I remember seeing him meet someone there a few days ago," Michael had to be extra careful not to reveal that he'd taken Jess on a stakeout with him that day instead of bringing her directly to the cabin as Tom directed. A mistake that almost cost her life.

"I just thought you should know. Jessie told me about how things were between you two, and it doesn't take a brain surgeon to see that you still love her." Tom's words hit Michael in the face. He knew the feelings he had for Jess were still there, but he wasn't sure he would call it love.

"I appreciate you letting me know what you found." Michael didn't know what else to say. This was not a conversation he wanted to have while lying on a hard couch with his head hurting the way it was.

"Anyway, I think you three need to come into the station, and we'll bring Hayden in for questioning," Tom ordered.

"Yes sir." Michael hung up the phone, dropping it back onto the floor where it had been sitting before Tom's call.

He looked over to see Harry curled up on the floor in a sleeping bag. He felt sorry for him, lying on the hard floor all night. Harry let out a snore, indicating he hadn't lost any sleep over the fact that he'd lost the coin flip for the couch. Michael rubbed the sore muscle on his shoulder. The couch probably wasn't any better than the floor. After taking a moment to stretch, he went to the bathroom to take a much-needed shower. It took a few washes to get the blood and dirt off the back of his head. The warm water seemed to ease his sore muscles. He'd be back in tip-top shape after a quick cup of coffee. After drying off, getting dressed, and giving himself a speed shave, he exited the bathroom to find Harry and Jess awake and dressed. They were each holding ceramic mugs.

"The coffee just got finished. There's some left if you want it." Jess pointed into the kitchen but kept her big brown eyes locked on his face. He strained to keep from smiling back at her.

How could he remain focused on the case if he melted every time she looked at him? Michael pushed the warm feeling in his chest away. No time to think about her sparkling chocolate eyes or her shiny, raven-black hair.

After making his cup, he joined the other two in the living room.

"So, what's on the agenda for today?" Harry asked with a hint of enthusiasm.

Michael took a sip from his cup before he replied. "I got a call from Tom this morning. He said he was able to figure out who the receipt belonged to."

"That was fast," Jess said.

"He said it belonged to Hayden Cunningham."

Jess's jaw dropped open. "My boss? I don't understand."

Her gaze dropped to the floor. He could tell by her slight frown that she was muddling it over in her mind to make sense of it. But if he explained it, Harry would know that he and Jess went on the stakeout they weren't supposed to go on. Would it somehow get back to Tom? He could lose his job over it. Still, Jess needed to know what he knew.

He watched her expression change as he explained what he saw in the deli on the day they were parked outside the maintenance worker's house.

"I was watching the house with binoculars the entire time you were there. He walked right by me, and I didn't see him." Jess took a gulp of her coffee. The fear in her eyes made him want to wrap his arms around her and pull her close to his side like he used to when she would get overwhelmed.

"There's more," Michael continued.

Both Harry and Jess stared at him, waiting for what he was about to say.

"He was talking to someone. I didn't see who it was, but it could've been the killer."

"Why didn't you tell me?" Jess asked.

"I didn't know it was Hayden. And... I don't know. I guess I didn't want to scare you," Michael explained as Jess stood.

She took Harry's now empty mug into the kitchen. Michael thought it was best to continue with Tom's instructions instead of getting into any sort of argument in front of Harry. It was better than sitting here in awkward silence. He knew Jess was angry with him.

"Tom wants us all to go to the station. They're gonna bring Hayden in for questioning to see what he knows. I suggest you get your things together." Michael took the last gulp of his coffee, set the cup in the sink, then went to pack his things.

*****

The ride back to town was silent. Michael drove while Harry sat in the back, watching the world go by. Jess had her arms crossed over her chest as if closing herself off from any conversation. Michael wished he could think of something to say that would get her to explain why she was upset.

They finally had a prime suspect. Their first big break in days. He would be glad when this case was put to rest. The open cornfields turned to farms, then to stores, as they got closer into town. They were less than five minutes from the OSPD, approaching the town square.

When he brought the car to a stop at the four-way intersection, he noticed there wasn't a lot of traffic today. As the light above their heads turned green, Michael stepped on the accelerator. He was already in the middle of the intersection when he heard the squealing brakes of the green Ford pickup that was speeding toward them.

Before he could remember where he'd seen it before, it slammed into the side of his truck, sending it barreling to the right. Jess screamed as his duffle bag in the back seat flew into the front. Michael gripped the steering wheel with all his might. He tried to guide them back onto the road, but the impact had sent them slamming into another car that was waiting to pass through the intersection.

It seemed like it took several minutes for the car to come to a complete stop. Michael's head started to hurt worse than it had the night before.

Not again. He grabbed his head and closed his eyes tightly, willing the pain and nausea to ease so he could check on Harry and Jess. He took long, deep breaths, trying to keep himself from vomiting. His stomach had just started to settle when his car door opened, and a firm hand gripped his shoulder. He opened his eyes to see Harry standing near his door.

"Hey, are you okay?" Harry asked.

"I'm not sure. I may have hit the sore spot on my head," Michael murmured. "How is it that you managed to get through that without a scratch?"

Harry's blurry figure shrugged. "Just luck, I guess. I don't know."

He grabbed Michael's shoulders, pulling him out of the vehicle.

Michael turned back just in time to see Jess's limp figure.

"Jess!"

Harry grabbed him. "She's unconscious. It looks like she's hurt pretty bad. I'd wait for the paramedics to get here before trying to move her. I think her leg is broken." He said.

Michael tried to remember at what point Harry was able to assess the situation and get all that information so quickly. His thoughts were a jumbled pile in his mind. He grabbed the left side of his head.

Harry's hand grabbed his shoulders once again. "I think you better sit down. You're both gonna need to go to the hospital."

No, he needed to check on Jess. He needed to see who it was that hit them.

"Did you check out the truck that hit us?" He wished he could make his way around the pile of cars to look at the truck, but he couldn't guarantee that he would be able to without falling. Not only did his head throb, but his legs felt like jelly.

"Yeah, a 2001 Ford pickup truck. Green." Harry stated.

"Are there rust spots over the right fender?" Michael asked.

"Hang on a sec. Let me go check." He disappeared and came back a few moments later.

"Yeah, just above the right fender. How'd you know?" Harry's voice had a tone of surprise.

"Because it looks like the truck that ran Jess and me off the road a few days ago," Michael explained. He only saw it for a few seconds before it slammed into them, but that was all it took for him to recognize it.

Michael's vision was still hazy when the ambulances arrived. He felt hands that weren't Harry's guiding him to a bright yellow object shaped like a gurney. Michael laid back on it. He knew that both Harry and Jess were in capable hands, but that didn't stop him from worrying about the driver of the green Ford pickup. There wasn't a doubt in his mind that this was no accident.

He could hear Tom's voice in the mix barking orders.

"Tom!" Michael called, praying he would hear him over the beeping horns of impatient traffic, loud voices, and the fire department cleaning up the mess of the demolished vehicles.

"Hey, Mike. How ya doing, bud?"

"That's him," was all he managed to get out before the world turned black.

CHAPTER 16

A sharp pain shot down Jess's leg. She couldn't move it. It seemed to be encased in something. She slowly opened her eyes to see that she was lying in a gray room with a white blanket pulled up to her waist. How did she get here? The last thing she remembered was driving to the police station with Michael and Harry.

"Hey, kiddo." A soft, familiar voice came from her left.

She tried to turn toward the voice, then winced in pain. Her entire body was extremely sore. She let her eyes focus until the figure sitting next to her bed became clear. Tom's mustached face formed a smile.

"What are you doing here? What's going on?" she asked.

"Well, you were in an accident. They brought you to Cincinnati General. You needed some tests that were a little too big for the clinic to handle."

"Michael," she whispered.

"He's got a pretty bad concussion. They've got him down the hall. I'm gonna go look in on him in a moment."

She pictured him lying in a hospital bed, surrounded by machines and tubes. This was all her fault. If only she knew how badly he was hurt. What if he died from his injuries? She'd never forgive herself.

Placing her open palms on the bed, she pushed herself upward, trying to find a more comfortable position, then whimpered, reaching for her leg.

"They said it's broken in a few places. You'll be out of commission for about eight weeks," Tom said.

"I wondered why it hurt so badly." She gritted her teeth. It was the worse pain she'd ever felt. "When can I get out of here?"

"They want to keep you for a few days for observation. I'm gonna go in a minute and let you get some rest, but there's something I want you to know first." Tom's face was difficult to read.

She could usually tell when he had good news or bad news. This time, his face seemed to be somewhere in between.

"Yes?"

Tom shook his head. "First, did you get a look at the vehicle that hit you?"

Jess knew he was trying to keep something from her. "Just spit it out, Tom!"

"Okay. Okay. We think we have the killer in custody." He stared at her as if waiting for a reaction.

She honestly didn't know how to react. Did they, or didn't they?

"What do you mean you 'think'?"

"We have to wait for you or Mike to ID him first. We're holding him for some unpaid speeding tickets," Tom explained.

"I can't identify him! I didn't see his face." She said as her insides trembled and twisted.

"Then we need to wait for Michael. They're only keeping him overnight."

He must not be hurt as badly as she was. She tried to hide that she was about to cry from relief. She didn't want to cry in front of Tom. Although she knew he would only try to comfort her. He'd been a great help to her since her mom passed away.

"You get some rest, Jessie." He patted her shoulder then closed the door on his way out.

She looked around the room to make sure she was alone. She needed time to think. Tom must've seen that everything that had happened over the last week was really taking its toll on her. Not only did her body ache from the car accident and from the several attacks, but her heart also ached as well. Michael was going through so much from his divorce. Being around her seemed to only make things worse for him. Maybe this was a sign that they weren't supposed to be together.

She hated that they stumbled into each other under the current circumstances. He wouldn't be in the hospital right now if it wasn't for her. He wouldn't have the gash on his head right now if it wasn't for her. She seemed to only bring bad luck to him.

All she wanted for him was happiness. He didn't need to be in a relationship so soon after everything he'd been through. She knew he still had feelings for her, or he wouldn't have kissed her. He probably did because he remembered how it used to be between them. She wasn't going to be anyone's rebound.

Jess hated to admit it, but she also had feelings for him. Even after the way he'd treated her. She couldn't put her finger on it, but there was something different about this Michael than the Michael she used to know. Had he grown that much in the last six years?

God allows things to happen to us to show us where we've gone wrong in our lives and how to set it right.

She had to smile when her mother's favorite saying echoed in her mind. Was that what was going on here? Was God trying to help her get her life back on track?

Life seemed to be going well for her in the last several years, or at least she thought so. Maybe it was *his* life that needed to be gotten back on track. Nothing seemed to be going right for him since she reentered the picture. Maybe if she stepped back out of his life, things would go better for him.

A tear rolled down her face. Letting go of him once again would rip out a piece of her heart that she may never recover from.

*****

Michael couldn't remember the last time he slept so well. He wasn't sure if he was really feeling better or if he was just imagining it. It was probably due to all the pain meds. The nurse told him they would knock him out. Boy, was she right.

After fastening the last button on his shirt, he laid the hospital gown on the tiny bathroom counter. It was nice to have regular clothes on. He'd only been in here overnight, but for some reason, it felt like he'd been here for weeks. Michael exited the bathroom, taking one more look around the midsize gray room to make sure he'd gathered all of his belongings.

He was anxious to get back to Oakwood Springs. He'd recognized the truck that ran into them, and he wanted to see what Tom had found on the guy. This had to be him.

He was just about to leave with his discharge papers in hand when the nurse stopped him. She was pushing a wheelchair.

"I don't need that," Michael said.

"Sorry, hun. It's hospital policy. You're a concussion patient," she explained. He hesitated, then seated himself. It felt strange to be pushed down the hallway when he was perfectly capable of walking.

As his chair glided down the hallway, he caught sight of Jess's room. An officer from the CPD was seated just outside her door. He wanted to peek in and see how she was doing, but she was probably sleeping.

He passed her door, nodding at the officer. Was he doing the right thing by leaving her?

"Just a second," He held his hand up for the nurse to stop pushing the chair.

A few nurses walked passed them along with a middle-aged woman whose eyes were red-rimmed. He turned to get one last look at Jess's hospital room door. Maybe he would peek in for a moment just to see if she was awake. Before he could tell the nurse to turn him around, another nurse entered Jess's room.

"Is something wrong, sir?" The nurse behind him asked.

"No..sorry." He gestured forward, causing her to resume pushing him.

The accident played out in his mind as he descended to the ground floor. The speed of the car, the impact, spinning out of control. He remembered Jess unconscious in the seat next to him. He was still pretty sore, but her injuries looked so much worse. It didn't matter anyway. If she was awake, she would still probably be angry with him for keeping information about the case from her. She had the right to be angry at him. He could never seem to make good decisions when she was involved.

As the elevator doors opened, Michael's phone vibrated in his pocket. He pulled it out and read the tiny screen. Carl Simpson's name appeared across it.

He slid the indicator to answer it. "Carl, what's up?"

"Hey Mike. Sheriff Cook told me you were being released from the hospital today. I thought I'd see if you needed a ride back to Oakwood Springs," Carl answered.

"Uh, yeah, actually,"

"I'm just about there. Watch for my car so you can just hop in, and we can get on the road." Carl said before he hung up the phone.

When Michael entered the hospital lobby, the sunlight pouring through the massive windows was almost blinding. He could see a few cars parked just outside the sliding doors. A nurse was helping an old man from a wheelchair into the passenger side seat. Another car was waiting for a young pregnant woman to climb out. The wide-eyed smile she flashed at Michael told him she was probably in labor.

"My ride is almost here." He told the nurse.

"I don't mind waiting with you," She responded with a smile.

It only took about two minutes for Carl's blue Camaro to appear at the entrance. He pulled up next to the doors. The nurse pushed him through them. Once they were next to the car, Michael stood.

"Thank you," he said, then climbed into the car. He would be glad when he was back in Oakwood Springs. Cincinnati was a great city and a nice place to live, but he had come to prefer small-town life.

He'd said goodbye to Cincinnati when his divorce was finalized. He felt like he should miss the secluded life he'd made for himself in Oakwood Springs, but he didn't. What he really wanted, what he craved, was what he felt when he was walking through the woods with Jess. Despite everything in his world spiraling out of control, she appeared just in time and seemed to make it all okay.

"Glad to see you got through the accident in one piece," Carl commented.

Michael was pulled back to reality. "Yeah, it was pretty bad. Especially after getting whacked over the head the night before last."

"I heard about that too. I'm supposed to talk to the guy who hit you. We think he might have something to do with the Tammy

Lenore case. His car was seen in the area on the night of her attack," Carl explained.

"If that's the case, then there's a good chance we've got Annabelle Mason's murderer." A flicker of hope ignited in his chest.

Jess would be safe. Now that he knew where she lived, he would be able to check on her now and then. Maybe even say hello.

Wait. He was getting a little ahead of himself. They weren't even sure that this was the killer or the accomplice. They needed irrefutable evidence that this guy murdered Annabelle and attacked Tammy, Jess, and him.

"There's something else I wanted to talk to you about," Carl added.

Michael stared at him for a moment, waiting for him to continue.

"You know my partner, Ed?" Carl asked.

"Yeah." He knew Ed and Carl were good friends as well as partners.

"Ed is retiring, which is gonna leave an opening for a new detective. I think you'd be a great fit."

Michael let Carl's words settle between them. He'd always wanted to be a detective. There weren't very many openings for that kind of job when he graduated with his degree in criminal justice. He'd settled for sergeant at the Cincinnati PD. After he left town, a deputy sheriff was the next best thing he could find. It hadn't mattered to him at the time. He just needed to leave Cincinnati behind.

Michael bit the inside of his cheek. "I'll have to think about it."

CHAPTER 17

Jess shifted and squirmed in the hospital bed, trying to move to a more comfortable position without sending pain shooting up her leg. She'd tried about five times in the last few hours without success. The orange and red light peeking into the room around the gray curtains told her that evening was settling in. Tom said Michael would try and identify the man he'd spoken to in the woods on the day of Annabelle's murder.

Hopefully, he could remember what the guy sounded like. He'd been hit over the head quite a bit lately, and that had to do quite a number on his memory. He should be able to tell if it was him by his body type and hair color. Little sprigs of silver hair had been peeking out from under his baseball cap.

She'd probably be dead right now if Michael hadn't shown up when he did that day. He stepped in and took charge when she told him what she saw. He was exactly what she'd needed at that moment. Her mind settled on Michael's tanned face.

Had he been released yet? She thought he would've at least stopped in to say hi. No. Michael had no obligation to her.

Remember that.

It was so easy to feel safe around him. At his house, at the police station, and even at the cabin. The ghosts of what it felt like to be his girlfriend lingered in her heart. She had to get a grip. Protecting her was just part of his job. It wasn't like he was there because he felt the same.

Maybe it was for the best that he didn't stop by. It would be better for him if they never spoke again. Tears welled up in her eyes and overflowed down her cheeks

Forget him, Jessica.

*****

Thanks to Carl and his speedy Camaro, Michael was able to make it back to Oakwood Springs around lunchtime. He was growing anxious to meet with the suspect and interrogate him. Part of Tom's plan was to spot any indication that the suspect recognized him from the conversation in the woods. If not, then they could explore the possibility that this was the accomplice. Perhaps the other man from the cornfield was simply the driver, but they wouldn't know for sure until evidence was found or someone confessed.

"Here we are," Carl's voice cut into his thoughts, pulling him back to reality.

Michael looked out his window to see that they'd stopped in front of the Oakwood Springs PD.

"That was fast." Michael realized he didn't remember a lot of the trip.

"Not really. You've been staring at the dashboard for the last hour and a half. I asked you what you were thinking about, but you didn't answer, so I left you alone."

"Sorry about that. Are you coming in, or is there somewhere else you need to be?" Michael asked.

"I'm gonna park the car, and I'll be in. If this is the guy who killed that girl, then he might be our guy as well," Carl explained.

Of course. How had the assault case slipped his mind all of a sudden?

"Sure. Thanks for the ride, though." He climbed out of the sports car. Michael often considered buying a car like this one. He would then change his mind whenever Carl let him ride in it, remembering how comfortable his pickup truck was and why he preferred it.

He entered the red brick building and took a deep breath. Why was he nervous? He'd never been nervous about questioning anyone before. He took a sharp right down the long hallway that led to the interrogation room. Tom was supposed to be there waiting for him.

"Michael! Great to see you back on your feet." Harry trotted down the hallway after him, carrying some files under his arm.

"Hey! Glad to see you weren't hurt in the accident." Michael scanned him. There didn't seem to be one bandage, bump, or bruise on him.

"Yeah. Lucky for me that the damage to your truck was mostly on the front. Actually, the passenger door pretty much came off on its own while they were trying to get Jess out," he said.

"Like they were aiming for it," Michael said, thinking out loud.

The expression on Harry's face changed from happy to see him, to sober. "Yes, actually. Tom said that same truck tried to run you guys off the road?" Harry asked.

"Yeah, I'd be shocked to find out that this guy isn't somehow involved in the murder. What do we know about him?"

Harry pulled one of the files out from under his arm and opened it. "I was just putting this together when you came in. The driver's name is Chester Beckman. He's sixty-five years old. He tried to say that he borrowed the truck from a friend, but the registration is in his name." Harry chuckled.

"Kind of a weird thing to claim. So he didn't think we'd check to see who the truck was actually registered to?" Michael asked with a twinge of concern.

Beckman was definitely lying, but it didn't prove that he was the killer or the accomplice. He wished the small amount of doubt would disappear from his stomach. They had their guy. Right? He wanted to believe that, but he'd also experienced being framed firsthand. It wasn't something he wanted off the table...yet.

"I don't know what he's thinking. He doesn't know that we know this is the truck that tried to run you guys off the road or that his truck can be tied to the Mason murder. Tom only informed him that the truck had been involved with some traffic violations—which Beckman also denies. Tom wanted to wait until you got here to ID him before moving forward with anything."

Michael propped his hands on his hips and let out a frustrated breath. "Thanks. Anything else?"

"Just one more thing. The address on the vehicle registration matches the one of the maintenance worker. I went over there this morning and found the jumpsuit in one of his garbage bins, just like the one Marge described."

"So we've pretty much got him," Michael deduced. Something didn't feel right about this. It was as if everything was coming together a little too easily.

"I guess so." Harry turned and disappeared into a room across the hall.

Michael continued on his way to the interrogation rooms. When he entered, he found Tom standing with his arms crossed, staring at the older man sitting in a small room at a table. Tom's head snapped in the direction of where he stood.

"I'm glad you're here." He dropped his arms to his sides, excitement in his eyes.

"What's going on?" Michael glanced through the two-way mirror into the interrogation room.

An older man wearing a baseball cap sat in a chair, handcuffed to the oak table in front of him. He was looking directly at Michael. He knew that could only be a coincidence. Still, he felt like Chester was planning how he would take care of him.

"Harry said you were waiting for me to get here before you interviewed him?"

"No, I want you to go in there and conduct the interview. It'll give you a chance to see if you recognize him. Maybe even get a confession, if we're lucky." Tom put a hand on his shoulder and pushed him toward the door.

"Okay, okay." Michael pulled away from his grip. His stomach tightened.

Interrogating a suspect was nerve-racking enough. If he said anything out of line or acted unprofessionally, a killer could go free. That was the last thing he wanted. He'd never interviewed a suspect in a case he was involved with before. He had to be careful.

He pushed open the door. "Hello, Mr. Beckman. My name is Officer Redman."

Chester pointed at him. "Hey, aren't you one of the people that was in the car I hit?"

"I'll be the one asking the questions." Michael took the seat across from him, anger growing in his stomach.

This was the guy he spoke to in the woods—the one who'd been coming after Jess. He took a deep breath. It was all he could do to keep from reaching across the table and knocking him right out of his chair.

"Are you aware that your vehicle has been spotted at the scene of several crimes that have taken place in the past few weeks?" Michael asked.

"They told me about some traffic violations or something," Chester mumbled. He must've known that Tom checked the registration on the vehicle and knew it was, in fact, his.

"Where were you last Friday night at nine thirty p.m.?" Michael asked.

"I was probably coming home from work," Chester replied.

"Where do you work?"

"I do maintenance jobs all over town."

"Have you ever done any maintenance work at Safe Haven?"

Chester's eyebrows formed a V on his forehead as he placed his palms flat on the table. "What's this have to do with traffic violations?"

Michael rolled a lot of routine questions around in his mind. He could go through each one of them, but there wasn't a doubt in his mind that this was the guy from the woods—the one who tried to kill Jess. The one who brutally murdered Annabelle Mason.

"Did you really think I wouldn't recognize your voice?" Michael finally said.

Chester's jaw twitched.

"I know who you are. I know you tried to kill Jess Everett. What I really want to know is why you killed Annabelle Mason and who you were with last Friday night." Michael explained.

Chester stared at him for a moment, then gave a small smile. "You think you've got it all figured out, don't you?"

His sudden tone change sent a chill down Michael's spine.

"If I don't, why don't you enlighten me?" He glared right back at Chester.

He couldn't help but feel like this was a showdown, like the western movies his dad watched when he was a kid.

"You probably think I killed Annie over drugs," Chester began.

"So you knew the victim."

"Victim?" He scoffed. "She liked to pretend she was a victim. She was just like her mother. Stubborn. Opinionated."

"You're her father."

"Stepfather, actually. A mistake I quickly corrected. Jessie girl can vouch for that."

Chester chuckled.

He slowed his breathing, trying to keep himself as calm as possible. He couldn't lose his temper on this guy no matter how badly he wanted to. People like Chester Beckman had no business walking around free.

"Who are you working with?" Michael repeated.

"I was hired to do this, but you'll not likely find him, so telling you is pointless." Chester's smirk irritated him more than the game he was playing.

"Either way, you're going to be charged with the murder of Annabelle Mason and the attempted murder of Tammy Lenore. As well as breaking and entering and assault and battery of Jess Everett. Oh, and not to mention assaulting a police officer." He added as he stood.

Chester said nothing in response, staring at him with hollow black eyes.

"This is your last chance to tell us who you're working for. We might be able to get the DA to cut you a deal." Michael waited a few seconds, his hand on the door, hoping Chester would spill his guts for a deal.

When a criminal knew they were caught, they would say or do anything to make things easier for themselves. Throwing anyone under the bus, they could. Chester just stared at him. The look in his eye said that he was hiding something else. Something vital to this case.

"Suit yourself." Michael exited the room with a shrug.

When he returned to the observation room, he found Tom standing with his arms crossed once again.

"Not exactly how I would've handled it, but effective nonetheless." Tom's expression was no longer excited.

It was easy to see that some of the things Chester said made him angry as well.

"What are we gonna do about the other guy?" Michael asked.

Tom dropped his head, focusing on the floor for a moment. He could almost see the wheels turning in his head as he processed everything to make the best decision possible. Even though he hadn't known him for very long, he had to admit that Tom was a great leader.

"We don't know for sure that the other guy is also out to kill Jess. He had the opportunity at the cabin and didn't take it," Tom said.

"But what if he is? Something could've messed up his plans,"

Michael wanted to get back to the hospital as soon as he could. First, to tell Jess they got Annabelle's killer, and secondly because his heart ached from being away from her for so long. But that was something he wasn't ready to tell her. He had to be sure it was the right moment.

"If he is, then Jess will need to remain in protective custody until we catch him," Tom replied.

"On it," Michael replied, rushing out the door before Tom could stop him.

CHAPTER 18

Michael slowly opened the door to the hospital room. He didn't know if Jess would be awake or not, so he'd be as quiet as he could just in case she was asleep. He was almost trembling with anticipation. She would be so relieved to know they caught Annabelle's killer.

He hoped she would be awake and feeling better. He remembered how groggy he felt this morning when he woke up. The pain killers he took worked wonders, but they kept him tired all day. He really wasn't supposed to be working with his injuries, but he would see this promise to Jess through. He was going to make sure she was safe before taking any time off.

A long curtain hanging from the ceiling kept her from view of anyone passing by in the hallway. They'd had a guard posted outside her room when he was discharged yesterday. They must've gotten the news that the killer had been caught, and she no longer needed police protection.

Michael thought it was strange that the police officer would leave the chair posted outside her room so quickly. He peeked around the curtain to see her staring toward the window. He had no idea what she was looking at since the curtains were closed.

"I can open those if you like. Let a little sunshine in here," He offered.

Jess turned her head toward him, giving him a slight twitch of the corner of her mouth, which he guessed was supposed to be a smile. Her black hair was loose and surrounded her head like a dark halo. She had a small cut over her eye that looked like it had been stitched up. Her eyes looked almost hollow.

"How are you feeling?" He asked, concerned.

She let her gaze drift to the floor and clenched her jaw as if not wanting to answer. He wished he knew what to say that would make her feel better. He began with the only thing he could think of. Something he should've said a long time ago.

"I'm sorry," he mumbled.

Her eyes shot up to look at him. "For what?"

"Everything. I was supposed to protect you, and I failed." He held her gaze.

Those dark brown eyes used to look back at him full of love. Now, they were filled with pain and abandonment. Something he was one hundred percent responsible for.

"You couldn't have protected me when you were unconscious." Jess squirmed in the narrow bed.

She winced, moving the white blanket aside that was draped over her legs to reveal a large cast that went from her hip to the tips of her toes.

"I mean before that," Michael said.

"You were working on the case."

"I mean... when we broke up." Part of him wished he could take back those words. No.

Even though it was a very uncomfortable topic they had both been avoiding, it was something she needed to hear. Whether she liked it or not.

"It's in the past. Besides, I'm better off alone." Her fingers played with the corner of the bedsheet.

"No one is better alone."

Jess tilted her head downward, her chin up against her chest and her hair falling around her face. She pushed it back behind her ears.

"Why did you come here, Michael?" she asked pointedly.

Now he was really regretting this conversation. He should've waited until he was sure she would forgive him and maybe give him the chance to prove that he wasn't a shallow jerk.

"I was able to identify the guy that hit us. He killed Annabelle Mason. His address was the same as the maintenance worker that attacked you when we were at Safe Haven. We found that jumpsuit in the garbage bin just outside of the house. Also, we found your car in his garage." Michael explained.

A single tear fell from her eye. "And Tammy?"

"I don't have the details on that, but I've known Detective Simpson a long time, and I know he'll get a confession out of the guy."

Jess leaned back in the upright bed, relief clear on her face. He wished he could leave her in the state of peace she seemed to drift into.

"We've got the killer, but he indicated that someone hired him to kill Annabelle. We don't know who that is yet, but I feel confident that it's the other man that was in the cornfield," He added.

Jess's face quickly changed from relief back to concern and fright. "I thought this had something to do with the drug dealer."

"We didn't find anything that would indicate this guy is involved with the drug ring. Plus, remember that night we were being chased by the pickup truck? There were two men in the car." Michael sat down on the corner of the bed, careful not to bump her leg.

"Jess, I'm sorry." He reached out for her hand.

She quickly jerked it back. "If that's all, then you've done your job. Please go."

"Jess." He tried again. There were still so many things he wanted to say to her before he stepped out of her life for good.

"Just go!" She swiped her hand toward the door.

Michael pressed his lips together. She wasn't going to forgive him. How was he supposed to let go of the heaviness he'd been carrying for the last six years? The guilt nearly took his breath away every time he thought about their last conversation. Her sobs as she begged him not to leave her. He hadn't even given her a chance to explain.

He could only imagine how she must've felt every time his phone went to voicemail when he hit the ignore call button. Jess had lost both of her best friends at the same time. There was no way she would've known how jealous Tiffany was of her. She really was left alone.

Michael scooted off the bed. Making his way to the door, the weight of the guilt grew twice as heavy. He wasn't sure if it was because he knew she would never forgive him for how quickly he wrote her off or if it was because he'd failed her once again.

"Just so you know, letting you go was the biggest mistake of my life." He stared at her for a moment, letting his words settle between them.

Would she pick up on what he was trying to imply? Why couldn't he say it? He loved her.

Coward.

＊＊＊＊＊

The days seemed to linger and the nights dragged by for the entire time she was in the hospital. But the worst part was being left to ponder the last thing Michael said to her. He'd regretted how things ended between them. She'd once longed to hear an apology, but he never actually said he was sorry until then. He'd apologized to her twice that day, but it wasn't as gratifying as she thought it would be. In fact, the whole conversation just made her feel worse.

The empty and alone feeling she'd carried left a hole in her heart. One that felt like it was growing bigger since Michael's hospital visit. Maybe it was simply because she'd spent the last few days in this room. She'd feel better when she was at home. Although she wasn't sure, she would feel totally safe there either. Getting back to how her life was before all this happened seemed nearly impossible.

As the time for her discharge got closer, she thought less about Michael and his regret. Her mind lingered on the fact that she was returning to a place that had been ransacked by a killer.

"I brought your discharge papers. I bet you're ready to get out of here," A nurse chirped, handing her a neat stack of papers stapled together.

Jess took the papers from the nurse. "Oh, yes. I never want to see this room again."

The nurse let out a musical chuckle as she guided her into a wheelchair. She handed Jess a pair of crutches to hold across her lap while she was being pushed down toward the elevator. It would be so nice to be outside and smell a cool breeze from nature instead of the antiseptic smell of the hospital air conditioning.

She felt awkward being pushed down the hall, getting sympathetic glances from each person that gazed down at her. She was tired of the sympathy. It was all she'd received from people since her parents died. When they finally made it to the doors that led outside, she saw an Oakwood Springs police cruiser waiting for her. Tom stood next to the passenger door, holding it open for her as if he was a uniformed chauffeur.

Good ole' Tom. He was the only person she could count on for the last six years.

"Ready to go?" He said with a smile.

She returned his smile, relieved to see something familiar. Something safe. "Absolutely."

The ride home was long, and her hip grew sore sitting sideways in the back of Tom's car. He wasn't comfortable putting her back there at first, but they didn't have much choice since she couldn't bend her knee. A twinge of anxiety hit her stomach when he turned into the parking lot of her apartment complex. She was home. It would take some getting used to because she hadn't been here in a few weeks. Tom pulled into the parking spot she usually parked in, turned off the engine, and climbed out.

"When do you think I'll get my car back?" Jess asked as Tom helped her out of the back seat.

"They're still going through it. We have all the evidence we need to convict Chester Beckman of the murder, but we're making sure there isn't anything that could point us to who was working with him."

Jess winced as she lowered her broken leg to the ground. Pain shot up her hip.

"It's not like you'll be needing it anytime soon," Tom added.

Jess began hobbling up the stairs to her apartment with an arm around the back of Tom's neck. She stood on her good leg as he unlocked her door. She peeked over her shoulder at the staircase behind her, which seemed a lot steeper all of a sudden. Visions of falling filled her mind, causing her to tighten her grip on Tom.

"There we go." He finally pushed the door open.

She hopped into her apartment, still gripping his shirt. Books, papers, and clothes were everywhere, along with the furniture that had been overturned. It was still a mess. She'd hoped that by some magic, it would have been cleaned up by now. She hadn't been here since just after Tammy's attack.

"Don't worry about all this," Tom said.

"There really isn't anything I can do about it right now anyway." She laughed nervously.

Tom handed her the crutches he'd carried up the stairs under his arm. She used them to steady herself while he flipped her recliner right side up. She backed up to it and plopped down into the plush chair. It was so much better than that hospital bed she'd spent the last five days in. She might even sleep in this chair tonight.

"Is there anything else I can get you?" Tom handed her the TV remote.

"Just a glass of water. You'll find the glasses in the first cabinet to your left." She pointed into the kitchen.

In a few seconds, she was drinking the best ice water she'd had in a long time.

"You sure you'll be alright on your own?" Tom asked her for the fifth time today.

"Absolutely." She took in a deep, relaxing breath.

"Alright, I'll come back tomorrow to check on you. We can get this place cleaned up then," Tom promised.

She smiled and waved to him as he disappeared through the doorway. She heard his footsteps slowly fade. That was one thing she loved about living here. She didn't need a doorbell because the apartment would vibrate every time someone would make their way up the stairs.

Jess turned on the TV, flipping through the channels to see if there was anything good on. She kept pressing the button until she went through every channel, finally settling on an old black and white movie.

It was an attempt to get her mind off the horrific events of the last few weeks. How did Chester Beckman find out she was in Oakwood Springs? Was it a coincidence, or had he been keeping tabs on her for all these years? He hadn't seen her since she was thirteen. Yes, he could've gone back to where she'd grown up and asked around. Her parents hadn't been gone that long, so their friends would still have a lot to say about them.

But she'd told her parents not to tell anyone where she lived. She'd come to Oakwood Springs after graduating college. She came here to leave the past behind her. To leave Michael behind her. She used to feel like she'd done a good job of that until discovering he'd done the same thing.

She thought about the moment she crawled out from under the bush where she'd been hiding from Chester. The moment she locked eyes with Michael. The flutter she felt in her heart. All the bittersweet memories came back to her at once. She wanted to forget about Michael because of how they broke up. How badly he'd broken her heart. But you couldn't really forget about someone you still loved. Jess blinked quickly, willing herself not to cry, but two big salty tears fell from her eyes anyway.

She'd imagined so many times what she would say to Michael if she ever bumped into him again. It was a game she would play with Tammy sometimes when the topic of heartbreak came up. She thought for sure she would feel pure satisfaction, especially if he tried to apologize. But now that she'd basically told him to get lost, she felt something she never expected. The same thing Michael said he'd felt for all these years. Regret. It had only been a few days since she'd seen him. She couldn't imagine feeling this way for years the way he had.

She wondered if she would've given him the chance to be friends if she'd run into him in another scenario. Would she have given him a piece of her mind like she imagined? All she knew was right now, she was miserable without him.

Jess glanced at the front door, remembering the night he brought her here to grab a few things. She was so overridden with fright that she didn't realize how much worse it could've been. Especially if she'd been here alone. The only reason she even made it out of this situation alive was because of Michael.

She leaned over, wiggling her phone from her pocket. Should she call him and tell him how miserable she was?

You're setting yourself up for another heartbreak. Seeing him again under the circumstances made her see how much she still loved him and what an amazing person he'd become.

But that was how God worked, wasn't it? He used the bad to bring good things into our lives. He let us go through trials to make us stronger. Those were some of the lessons she remembered from Sunday School when she was a child. It never really made sense to her until now. Yes, she learned that God used the bad to bring the good, but what if the good would never speak to her again.

Jess scanned the room, unable to focus on the movie. She got a sick feeling every time she caught sight of the mess made in her apartment. It was a reminder that this place wasn't as safe and secure as she once thought. She turned off the TV. There was no way she would get any rest as long as this place remained the disaster it was.

She leaned up from the recliner, using one of her crutches to pull herself to her feet. It took a minute to hobble into the kitchen and grab one of her dining chairs. She adjusted the crutch under her arm so she could inch along, squeezing it with her armpit while pulling the kitchen chair behind her.

The easiest place for her to start was the bookshelf. Why he felt the need to knock every single book off made no sense to her. Several minutes later, she finally settled in the chair in front of the bookshelf. She leaned over, picked them up two at a time, and started arranging them back on the shelf in the order she had them before. She liked arranging the books by the color of their covers. Each book contained a memory. A lot of them had been Christmas and birthday gifts from Michael.

She'd gotten the first shelf completed and picked up a few books to start the second shelf when someone knocked on the door. Goosebumps formed over her arms. Nobody called to check and see if she was home yet. Maybe someone heard about Chester's arrest and assumed she'd be home now that the killer was apprehended.

There were two men in the car. Michael's words from the hospital echoed through her head. Maybe she should pretend she wasn't home. Why hadn't she heard anyone coming up the stairs? Were they trying to sneak up on her? Jess grabbed the crutch from the floor next to her and pulled herself to her feet. A second knock, a little harder this time, echoed through her apartment.

"Just a minute," she called.

There was no turning back now. Whoever was out there now knew she was here. She hopped to the door and peered through the peephole. Terrified of who she might see on the other side. She closed an eye and pressed her nose against the door to get a clear look. It was Hayden Cunningham.

Jess frowned, trying to think of some reason why Hayden would be paying her a visit. She didn't want to let him in because he was still a suspect and could very well have been the other man in the car with Chester. He was still technically her boss. But if he was involved, then she would have to play it cool. If he knew that she knew his dirty little secrets, she'd be in big trouble. Twisting the knob, she pulled the door open, pasting on a pleasant smile.

"Hayden, what are you doing here?" She said.

He didn't respond but pushed past her into her apartment and took a quick scan of the room. Immediately, alarm coursed through her. His towering figure went to the center of the living room.

"I just wanted to see how you were getting along." He shoved his hands in the pockets of his long coat. She'd never seen Hayden in casual clothes, but for some reason, he was in a black, long-sleeve shirt and dark blue jeans. His tone sent a shiver down her spine.

"How did you know I was home?" She sounded more suspicious than she meant to.

Hayden turned his gaze back to her. His eyes darted back and forth as if searching for an answer she would believe.

"I heard it from the sheriff's office. I just wanted to check up to make sure you're getting better. You've been missed at Safe Haven," he explained.

She didn't believe that answer at all. Tom said he hadn't told anyone she was discharged, not even Michael. Jess remained by the door with her one crutch tightly under her arm.

"Yeah, Sheriff Tom told me you've been asking about where I am and stuff," she said.

"Well yeah. One day you're at work. The next I hear that one of the Safe Haven women has been murdered, and you disappear." Hayden held up his hand in a questioning gesture.

Jess patted her side, hoping Hayden wouldn't notice that she was looking for her phone.

She caught sight of it still sitting on the arm of the recliner.

Darn!

"Well, I'm fine, and I'll let you know when I'm able to come back to work." She let the door swing open, hoping Hayden would take that as a cue for him to leave. But he didn't.

She hobbled back to the recliner and sat down, letting the phone fall between the arm of the chair and the cushion. She pretended to rest her hand on her thigh but used her knuckles to call Michael.

Hayden turned to face her. The movement of his body caused his jacket to whip around enough for her to spot a pistol tucked into his pants. She'd never known him to carry one before. Hayden must have noticed she'd seen the gun. He pulled it out and pointed it at her chest. Jess clenched her jaw. If she was going to die right here and now, she wasn't going to give him the satisfaction of seeing her afraid.

"You've poked your nose somewhere it doesn't belong, which is something you and your cop friend seem to be doing a lot of lately." Hayden's tone grew angrier with each word. "But I'm going to make sure it's a mistake you won't repeat."

CHAPTER 19

Jess couldn't remember a time in her life that she'd ever been more terrified than she was right now. She was sitting in her recliner in her apartment, and her boss was holding a gun in her face. He could pull the trigger at any moment, and it would all be over. She prayed Michael could hear everything Hayden said over the phone. She had it tucked deep between the cushion and the arm so Hayden couldn't see it.

"So you're just gonna kill me where I sit? I can't even run, you know. You aren't that cold-blooded, Hayden."

"I know. It'll make my job a lot easier, though. You don't know me as well as you think." He took a step closer.

Her mind was racing. There wasn't anything within reach she could use to defend herself. Hayden pulled back the hammer. Just before he squeezed the trigger, a pounding knock on the door snagged his attention.

Hayden's head whipped toward the door. He took a big frustrated sigh, shoving the gun back into its original resting place in his belt. He grabbed Jess by the arm and pulled her out of the chair. She whimpered as she put pressure on her broken leg to steady herself, then grabbed her crutch so she wouldn't totally lose her balance.

"Answer the door," Hayden hissed in her ear.

Jess scooted her way to the front door, trying her best not to cry from the excruciating pain in her leg. She knew Hayden well enough to know that he always finished what he set out to do. She hobbled toward the door, glancing back to the chair where her phone was, and praying it wouldn't be discovered. Jess opened the door to see a tall man with curly blonde hair wearing a backward ball cap. It was Jerrod. He took care of the bushes along the front of each apartment and occasionally did some repairs.

"Maintenance. I'm supposed to fix a hole in your wall or something." Jerrod had a few tools in his hand.

"How did you know about the hole in my wall? I never called about it," She asked.

"Aunt Mandy heard you were out of town and stopped in to check on your place. She told me about it," He explained. He was the last person she expected to see today, but she would take any way out of this situation she could get.

She clenched her jaw. If Hayden was ready to kill her a few seconds ago, what was he thinking now? She didn't know what to do. If she invited Jerrod in, he could be walking right into his demise. If she tried to signal him that she needed help, it could still result in both their murders.

She could try to send him away, but she needed help *now,* and a distraction could be the best thing for her situation. She peeked behind the door to see a glaring Hayden gritting his teeth and whipping his gun back and forth, signaling her to get rid of him. Before she could think of a good reason why now wasn't a good time for him to be drywalling, Jerrod pushed past her.

"It shouldn't take me too long," he said eagerly.

His great aunt Mandy always called him an eager beaver. This was one time she wished he wasn't so eager. Jerrod walked into the apartment, quickly spotting Hayden. She reached out to grab him and warn him but quickly jerked her hand back when she saw that Hayden had hidden his gun behind his back. Maybe he would at least let Jerrod walk out of here unharmed. He was only trying to do his job.

"I'm sorry for doing this while you have company, Ms. Everett, but I'm going on vacation next week and didn't think you wanted a huge hole in your wall for the next two weeks." Jerrod's apology was sincere.

Jess's heart was pounding so hard that she thought it was going to break her ribs. He was a good kid, but he wasn't very observant.

"It's alright. This is just my boss, Hayden Cunningham."

Telling Jerrod Hayden's name was a risky move, but if Hayden didn't kill him when he walked through the door, it wasn't likely he would at all. Unless he absolutely had to. Jess took a peek at Hayden. She hadn't noticed before, but she could see sweat forming on his forehead. Was he nervous?

Maybe that was something she could use to her advantage.

"Wow, That's a pretty big hole, Ms. Everett. What happened?" Jerrod stood and turned his gaze to Jess. He must not have heard about the killer chasing her.

She'd expected it to be all over town by now. Marge had been there the day she was attacked at Safe Haven. Marge was a dear lady, but when she got to talking around her friends, things would often be revealed that weren't supposed to be. Sometimes she didn't even realize she'd told something she wasn't supposed to until it was already out of her mouth.

"I'm not really sure."

Jerrod gave her a look that told her he wasn't satisfied with that answer.

"You can come back to fix it later," Hayden barked at him.

Jess shivered, praying Jerrod wouldn't leave before Tom or Michael showed up. Had he been listening this whole time? Had he hung up before hearing everything Hayden said about Annabelle's murder?

Where are you? She wasn't sure if she was referring to Michael or God. But she would accept either one intervening.

Jerrod stood, pulled a tiny notebook from his pocket, and scribbled a few times in it. "I'll get everything I need to make the repairs and be back tomorrow. Will that work for you?"

Jess tried to think of something she could say to get Jerrod to stay with her, but she couldn't. It wasn't fair to bring him into the middle of this mess. "That works."

He smiled, nodded, then left, waving to her as he closed the door behind him. Hayden turned toward her once again, pulling the pistol from his belt.

*****

Michael stared at his phone screen in confusion. Jess had called him. He'd answered and could hear voices but couldn't make out anything said. It didn't make any sense. After their conversation in the hospital, he didn't expect to hear from her again. She'd made her choice, and he would once again have to try to forget her while carrying the regret in his heart. The call could've been a pocket dial.

He tapped the red button and placed it back on his desk. The phone call was probably nothing, but Michael couldn't help but feel like there was something wrong. Just as he was about to turn his attention back to his computer and the stack of reports he had to fill out, Tom came through the door.

"Just took Jessie home. She should be settled by now," Tom told him.

"Thanks for letting me know. Was there anyone there with her when you left?" Michael asked.

Tom frowned in concern bringing two firm fists up to his hips. "No. Why do you ask?"

"I just got a call from her. I heard multiple voices in the background. At least one of them was a male."

Tom scratched his chin, pulling his flip phone from his pocket. He tapped it a few times, then placed it to his ear.

"She's not picking up," He said with concern.

"Maybe both of us should go back and check on her. Just in case. It may have been her TV, but we can't take any chances with our second perp still out there."

Michael grabbed his jacket as he stood to his feet.

"I was thinking the same thing." They made a dash for Tom's car. The siren wailed as they sped off in the direction of Chestnut Crest Apartments. This might be a false alarm, but an unwanted image appeared in his head of Jess lying on the floor in her apartment. His stomach twisted at the thought. He swallowed a lump forming in his throat before Tom noticed his distress. If only Jess knew how much he still loved her. He couldn't stand the thought of anything happening to her.

Tom drove the police car out of the parking lot and sped down the highway. As they got closer to the apartment, Michael considered all the evidence suggesting that Hayden was the other man in the car that night when he and Jess hid in the cornfield. If he was, how far would he be willing to go to get rid of her? It would also mean that he was the one that hired Chester.

Hayden was the son of the mayor and apparently didn't care much about his job, nor the people that worked under him, or Jess wouldn't have felt so threatened and uncomfortable by the conversations she had with him. Michael's blood began to boil. He had a few ideas of what he would do if Hayden hurt Jess in any way.

Finally, the sign for the Chestnut Crest Apartments came into view. His breath turned shaky when he caught sight of Hayden's car parked right next to the stairs leading up to her place. It was the same car parked directly behind him when he was sitting in front of Sam's deli with Jess. On the other side of Hayden's car was a large utility van that looked like it was full of tools.

A young man with blonde hair came down her stairs. He wore work clothes and had a tool belt around his waist.

Tom brought the car to a screeching halt behind Hayden's, just in case he tried to flee the scene. The team of officers both climbed out, pulling their pistols from their holsters. Michael hoped he wouldn't have to use it, especially not in front of Jess. He looked up at the top floor to see the curtain flutter as someone took a peek at them.

"Hey, what's going on?" The maintenance worker looked agitated that his van was blocked in too.

"What's your name?" Michael asked firmly.

"Jerrod. Jerrod Craft. Am I in trouble?" His expression changed from concern to fear.

Michael wasn't sure if he was involved in this somehow but couldn't take any chances. He pointed up to the window of Jess's apartment. "What were you doing in that apartment?"

Jerrod twisted his neck toward where he was pointing. "I'm supposed to be patching some holes in the wall, but Ms. Everett has company right now."

Michael shot a look at Tom, who was standing just behind him. Tom nodded back, confirming that their suspicions were correct. Jess was in danger.

Her car was nowhere in the parking lot. The only way Hayden would know she was home was if he'd been here waiting for her to arrive.

Please protect her, Lord. Michael knew he needed God on his side in this. It was Jess's only hope of surviving. The fact that she was still alive gave him hope that He was already working in her favor.

Michael grabbed Jerrod by the arm and pulled him to Tom's police cruiser. "Stay in here." He pushed Jerrod into the back seat and slammed the door before he could protest, then rushed back to rejoin Tom.

"The front steps are the only way in and out of the apartment." Tom looked up toward Jess's window and froze.

Michael looked back up at the window as well. The curtain was now pulled aside, and the window was open. There stood Hayden with a pistol in his hand, the barrel pointed directly at them.

"The first person who tries to come up those stairs will be dead before their foot hits the first step," he shouted at them.

Michael balled his fists. He could almost feel his knuckles turning white. He took a deep breath to control the rage quickly growing in his chest. He felt totally helpless. It was a feeling he knew well and one he hated more than anything.

"All I want is to get in my car and drive away. If you want to ever see Jess alive again, you'll stay out of my way," Hayden growled to cover the nervous vibrations in his voice.

Michael clenched his jaw. That could either work to their advantage, or it could cause Hayden to make a mistake and kill someone. He exchanged a look with Tom and gently placed their guns on the concrete sidewalk. Then both of them took a few steps backward.

"Go then. Nobody's stopping you," He shouted back.

Hayden disappeared from the window. Michael's mind raced, trying to come up with a plan to get Jess out of there and nab Hayden before he could escape. About thirty seconds later, her apartment door crashed open. He expected Hayden to appear with a gun pointed at him once again. What he saw caused his heart to lurch in his chest. Hayden held Jess around the waist, pointing the gun at her temple. The two of them slowly made their way down the stairs.

Michael's body tensed. It was all he could do to keep himself from lunging at Hayden, but he knew if he did, Jess would be dead before he got to them. Hayden stared at him, his eyes wide as saucers and the gun shaking in his grip.

He pulled her closer when they reached the bottom of the stairs. He was holding her up for the most part, her face wincing in pain with every step. It was a clever move. Without her crutches, Jess wouldn't be able to leave his grasp. Michael met her gaze. Her lips were trembling, and there were tears stains on her cheeks. The look of brokenness in her eyes was like a knife to his heart.

CHAPTER 20

Jess's heart pounded in her chest. Hayden tightened his hold around her waist. If she did end up dead, at least they would know who the murderer was this time.

Hayden was responsible for everything. He hired Chester to kill Annabelle. He was the one behind all the drug activity in Safe Haven. If Chester hadn't been caught in the accident, he would've killed her too, but now that was left for Hayden. Michael and Tom stood only a few feet away. They were positioned like cats, ready to pounce. They would let him escape to save her life, but what they didn't know was that he was lying. He had no intention of letting her live. She was being used as insurance for his escape.

That couldn't happen. Hayden deserved to go to jail for what he was doing to the girls in Safe Haven. He took advantage of their weak state. She was willing to lay down her life to ensure he wouldn't hurt anyone else. In time, every one of them who didn't do what he wanted would've ended up like Annabelle.

Jess let out a gasp, pretending it was from the pain, but it was the only way she could think to get Michael's attention. She gave him a small smile, then silently mouthed the words, *I forgive you.* His eyes grew wide. He'd gotten the message. After everything he'd been through, he deserved some peace in his life.

She hated what he'd done to her all those years ago—how badly he'd broken her heart—but she never truly hated him. What she hated was the fact that she never stopped loving him. But hate wasn't something she wanted anymore, especially if these were her last moments. She allowed her love for him to be released from the dark corner of her heart where it had been locked away.

"Hayden, you don't want to do this." Michael took one step toward them.

Hayden pulled the gun from her temple and pointed it at Michael. Jess didn't stop to think. She grabbed his extended wrist and gave him a firm elbow to the gut. He let out a growl as he released her waist.

She instinctively tried to keep herself from falling by catching herself on her broken leg. Excruciating pain shot through her like lightning. The world around her slowed down as she fell to the ground, expecting Hayden to fire his gun at any second.

Out of the corner of her eye, she saw someone else running up from behind Hayden. She caught sight of a pair of jeans and black shoes, but she hit the ground before she could see their face. There was a tussle behind her and a thud. Had they gotten him? Was it over? She pushed herself up off the ground, blood trickling from her palms from the hard concrete.

Tom lunged toward Hayden while another figure ran up behind him, pushing him to the ground. Michael whipped a pair of handcuffs from his pocket. In seconds, Tom was leading him to his car. Jerrod quickly climbed out of the back seat, and Tom pushed Hayden in.

Michael ran over to her, helping her to her feet. "Are you alright?"

She wasn't sure if she could stand. Her broken leg now felt numb. He quickly noticed she was having trouble standing and helped her up. She threw her arms around his neck and squeezed. Tom appeared with her crutches.

"I don't know," she whispered in his ear. She'd just gotten a lot closer to death than she wanted to think about.

Michael gave her a squeeze in return, which made a comforting warmth seep through her body. She felt complete with him. Whole. A feeling she only experienced when she was with him.

She looked over her shoulder to see Tom moving his squad car out from behind Hayden's car and Jerrod's van. Jerrod waved to Tom then pulled out of the parking lot, quickly disappearing from view. She was relieved to see that he was alright. The other man stood on the sidewalk, talking into a walkie-talkie. She instantly recognized him as the detective working on Tammy's assault case.

"What's he doing here?" Jess asked as he approached them.

Carl shook his head. "Good thing I happened to come outside when I did. Someone might have gotten hurt."

"You aren't kidding. You were in just the right place at the right time, but... what are you doing here?" Michael asked.

Carl blew out a big breath as if the tackle had taken a lot out of him. "My investigation led me here. I was trying to figure out who was responsible for bringing the drugs into Oakwood Springs."

"Looks like we both got our guy," Michael said with a smile.

"Um, no. That's not him," Carl looked at Michael as if he was crazy.

Michael's head jerked back as he frowned. "That's Hayden Cunningham. He's been trying to kill Jess for weeks now. He first hired a hitman. We got him. But today, he came here himself to finish her off."

Jess's stomach clenched when she heard the scenario spelled out. How many times could she have been killed? She'd lost count.

"Look, all I know is that the guy I'm trying to find is kind of young and blond." Carl pulled a notepad from his pocket. "Jerrod Craft is the name I got,"

Jess stared at Carl for a moment. She wasn't sure if what she'd just heard was real or if she'd imagined it.

Michael looked at her. "Who is Jerrod Craft?"

She blinked a few times, trying to get her mouth to form words. There had to be some mistake. She couldn't imagine Jerrod doing anything wrong, much less being a drug trafficker.

"He's the maintenance worker. His aunt owns the apartments," she quickly explained.

If Jerrod really *was* some kind of drug lord, then it made sense that his investigation would lead him here.

Carl seemed completely confused by their sudden revelation. "What am I missing here?"

"That van that just pulled out belonged to the guy you're looking for. C'mon. We can still catch him." Michael squeezed Jess's waist tighter as if he would carry her.

"No, you stay with her. I'll grab the sheriff," Carl commanded, running over to Tom.

He must've given him the quick version of the details because Tom pointed at his car. The two men climbed inside and sped off in the same direction the van had gone, taking a cuffed Hayden with them.

"No wonder Hayden didn't kill him," Jess said under her breath.

"What do you mean?" Michael's breath tickled her neck. She'd forgotten how close he was.

"I was afraid Hayden would hurt Jerrod. I tried to get rid of him. He seemed fine that he was there, and it was almost as if he was going to let him go. I didn't realize it was because he was intimidated by him." she explained.

"He was probably there to check up on Hayden. You noticed things at Safe Haven and quickly became a threat to their entire operation." Michael caressed her chin, tilting her head upward to face him. "Jess, did you say what I hope you said earlier?"

"I said, 'I forgive you,'" she said softly. For all the pain he caused her and all the pain he'd caused himself. She desperately wanted to put the past behind them.

"Why?" he whispered.

She held his gaze for a moment. She wasn't sure if he thought what he'd done wasn't forgivable or that he wasn't loveable.

"Because I love you. I always have. And I know now I always will." It felt so good to finally say it out loud.

"You don't know how long I've waited to hear those words from you." Michael pulled her into a long and meaningful kiss.

She fully understood what her mother's favorite saying meant.

God allowed things to happen to us to show us where we've gone wrong in our lives and how to set them right.

*****

Michael felt lighter than he had in years. He was in the back seat of Harry's cruiser with his fingers intertwined with hers. She loved him, and she'd forgiven him. That was all he needed.

"I can't believe it's over," Jess said as they made their way back to the police station.

"It's not quite over yet. We still need to get some answers and evidence to ensure these guys are put away for good." Michael looked over at her just in time to see a look of disappointment in her eyes.

"You'll have to do just as much work for this as I will," he continued.

"I'll do whatever I need to."

A little while later, they were sitting with Carl in Tom's office. Hayden made a full confession, giving them the last few pieces to the puzzle.

"We now know that Hayden hired Chester to kill Annabelle. She no longer wanted to be part of their scheme to sell drugs in town, which got her killed. Jess just happened to walk in as the murder was taking place. The crazy part is that he said he remembers Jess living next door to him. Annabelle saw him kill his wife, her mother, and he'd threatened to kill her if she told anyone," Tom explained.

"What a horrible thing to say to a thirteen-year-old." Jess squirmed in her chair.

Michael remembered what Jess told him about the guilt she carried from knowing her at that age.

"So, Jess was just at the wrong place at the wrong time?" Michael chimed in.

"Pretty much. Also, we haven't found any evidence to indicate that Linus Mason was involved in any way," Tom added.

Carl hopped off of the corner of the desk where he'd been sitting. "No, but there is a warrant out for him. I'm supposed to take him back to Cincinnati with me along with Jerrod Craft.”

"I'll send a few officers to help you transport them," Tom offered.

Carl smiled and nodded a thank you to Tom. As he left the room, Michael followed him.

"Thank you for all your help in this case." He gave him a firm pat on the back.

"No problem. Judging by the way you were looking at Ms. Everett, I can assume you won't be taking that position I mentioned before," Carl stated.

Michael didn't know it was that obvious. He smiled. "You assume correctly."

"I don't think I've ever seen anyone so happy to be missing out on a promotion," Carl said.

"Some things are more valuable," Michael replied.

If the position had been offered to him just two weeks ago, he might have taken it. But it was part of God's plan. It was as if all the years of pain and loneliness melted away. Jess was back in his life, and he would do whatever it took to make sure she remained there.

The scars on his heart could finally heal.

EPILOGUE

Six months later

Jess took the hand of a young woman who couldn't have been more than twenty-one. It was a typical case. The girl had been with her boyfriend since middle school. Things were going great between them up until the last few months. It was around the time they'd moved in together. She'd seen so many cases like this.

"He didn't mean it!" The girl sobbed as she watched her boyfriend being placed in the back seat of a police cruiser.

"Candice, listen to me. He's going to get the help he needs. This will be good for both of you in the long run. Andy needs help, and this is the only way he's gonna get it," Jess explained.

It was a speech she'd given to so many women in the county. They needed to know that this was not how life was meant to be lived, and it was okay to accept outside help. She wished that someone could've been there for Michael. She wasn't sure if she could do anything to help men in the country who could be dealing with the same thing, but with God's help and Michael's, she was certainly going to try.

Jess guided Candice to her car and helped her into the back seat. Candice buried her head in her hands, and Jess closed the car door and turned to see Michael approaching her.

"Do you think she'll press charges?" he asked.

"They usually don't. Most of them choose to move into Safe Haven while the significant other gets therapy or anger management. All we can really do is monitor the process."

Michael was still learning how this worked. He'd only just become Sherriff a few months ago when Tom decided to retire and recommended him for the job. The county appointed him the new sheriff until the next election. Then he could formally run if he still wanted the position.

Jess imagined Tom at his cabin, fishing and hiking through the woods in the cool of the morning. She missed working with him but knew he was happy to be out of law enforcement. She'd been given Hayden's job. One she hoped to never take for granted.

"Harry's gonna take Andy down to the station and handle everything. Are we still on for dinner?" Michael stared at her with a hopeful expression.

He'd looked at her that way ever since they started *dating* again. It still sounded strange whenever she said it out loud.

"Sure. I just need to take her to Safe Haven and make sure she gets settled," Jess explained.

He smiled at her, holding her gaze. She knew he would've kissed her if they weren't surrounded by other officers and EMTs. Thank goodness he knew better. Although it didn't matter. Everyone in town knew about their relationship.

"See you then." He threw her a wink as he turned to leave.

Jess sent a smile back. He said he had something special planned for the night and wouldn't tell her what it was. All she knew was that she was supposed to wear the new purple dress she'd just bought.

She circled the front of her car and climbed in. There was a girl in her backseat who needed to hear about the love and hope in Christ that Jess now finally understood.

*****

Michael nervously tapped his foot under the table. He'd gotten a reservation at the best Italian restaurant in town. Jess loved Italian food. He stuck his finger in the collar of his crisp blue shirt to loosen his tie. He looked up just in time to see Jess approach the table. Her hair was up in a twist on the back of her head. She had on the royal purple dress he'd asked her to wear. It came just below the knee and had slits in the sleeves that began on her upper arm.

"Having a little trouble with your tie?" she teased.

"Just not used to wearing one, is all." He chuckled nervously.

She hadn't seemed to catch on to what he had planned. She reached over and loosened his tie enough so that it was comfortable and no longer pressing up against his throat, then sat in the seat across from him.

"It's been a while since I've been here." She took a quick scan of the dining room.

Each table had a white cloth draped over it and maroon napkins folded over gold place settings.

"It's a step up from our normal dates." He said as he gave her a quirky smile, letting his shoulders bounce with a shrug.

Most of their date nights were spent at each other's houses, taking turns cooking for one another. He wasn't going to admit it, but he preferred that more than going out.

"Jess," he began, wanting to bring their conversation to the reason why he chose to come here for their weekly date before anything else was said. She turned her attention to him. Her brown eyes sparkled, pushing him to continue before he lost the nerve.

"Jess, I wanted to bring you here tonight to say that losing you was the worst mistake of my life and one that changed everything for the worse. I know now that my life without you doesn't make sense, and I hope to never lose you again." He took a deep breath before continuing. Her head tilted slightly to the side. He could see concern slowly forming on her face.

He reached into his pocket and pulled out a small black velvet box. "I want to ask you something I should've asked a long time ago. Will you be my wife?"

He opened the box, placing it in front of her. Her mouth fell open. She covered it with her hand, looking down at the opened ring box, then at him. Tears rolled down her cheeks. Michael held his breath, unable to imagine another second of his life without her in it.

Her dark brown eyes met his. "Of course! Yes!"

THE END

Rebecca Hemlock is an Award-winning author and has written articles, books, and short stories for many years. She has worked as a freelance journalist for 4 years. She is currently a member of Sisters in Crime and American Christian Fiction Writers. Her books have also made it to the Amazon.com #1 bestseller list several times.

Aside from writing Romance and suspense, Rebecca enjoys writing children's fiction. Her first children's book, The Lost Soldier, was published in 2016 by Westbow Press. She has a total of 3 children's books, all published under the name R.C. Burch from 2016 to 2017. Rebecca has earned a degree in English and an Appalachian Studies certificate in Creative Writing. Her favorite times to write are early in the morning when the sun is coming up and at sunset. Rebecca lives in Eastern Kentucky with her husband and children